MISS PERFECT

JILL ROSS KLEVIN

SCHOLASTIC INC.
New York Toronto London Auckland Sydney Tokyo

Cover Photograph by Don Banks

ISBN 0-590-32542-6

12 11 10 9 8 7 6 5 4 3 2 1   5   4 5 6 7 8/8

Printed in the U. S. A.   06

MISS PERFECT

A Wildfire Book

WILDFIRE TITLES FROM SCHOLASTIC

Love Comes to Anne by Lucille S. Warner
I'm Christy by Maud Johnson
Beautiful Girl by Elisabeth Ogilvie
Superflirt by Helen Cavanagh
Dreams Can Come True by Jane Claypool Miner
I've Got a Crush on You by Carol Stanley
An April Love Story by Caroline B. Cooney
Yours Truly, Love, Janie by Ann Reit
The Summer of the Sky-Blue Bikini
  by Jill Ross Klevin
The Best of Friends by Jill Ross Klevin
Second Best by Helen Cavanagh
A Place for Me by Helen Cavanagh
Take Care of My Girl by Carol Stanley
Lisa by Arlene Hale
Secret Love by Barbara Steiner
Nancy & Nick by Caroline B. Cooney
Wildfire Double Romance by Diane McClure Jones
Senior Class by Jane Claypool Miner
Cindy by Deborah Kent
Too Young to Know by Elisabeth Ogilvie
Junior Prom by Patricia Aks
Saturday Night Date by Maud Johnson
He Loves Me Not by Caroline Cooney
Good-bye, Pretty One by Lucille S. Warner
Just a Summer Girl by Helen Cavanagh
The Impossible Love by Arlene Hale
A Kiss for Tomorrow by Maud Johnson
Sing About Us by Winifred Madison
The Searching Heart by Barbara Steiner
Write Every Day by Janet Quin-Harkin
Christy's Choice by Maud Johnson
The Wrong Boy by Carol Stanley
Make a Wish by Nancy Smiler Levinson
The Boy for Me by Jane Claypool Miner
Class Ring by Josephine Wunsch
Phone Calls by Ann Reit
Just You and Me by Ann Martin
Homecoming Queen by Winifred Madison
Holly in Love by Caroline B. Cooney
Spring Love by Jennifer Sarasin
No Boys? by McClure Jones
Blind Date by Priscilla Maynard
That Other Girl by Conrad Nowels
Little Lies by Audrey Johnson
Broken Dreams by Susan Mendonca
Love Games by Deborah Aydt
Miss Perfect by Jill Ross Klevin

One

"There she goes. Miss Perfect," Billy Raines snickered as Kim sped down the corridor. She kept on going, pretending she hadn't heard him. Miss Perfect, the girl most likely to succeed at *everything* — the smartest, most talanted, and dedicated overachiever in the school. Recipient of honors awards for scholastic excellence; captain of the debating team; president of the drama club; the first junior ever to be editor-in-chief of the school newspaper; an accomplished singer, dancer, actress, and athlete. A cinch to graduate valedictorian from her class a year from June. Miss Perfect, alias Supergirl. All pluses, no minuses — at least that's what everyone thought. If they knew what it was like to be her, they wouldn't think so anymore.

She was a walking case of burn out, but what was a case of chronic fatigue in the

1

overall scheme of things? She was getting five or six hours of sleep a night when she needed eight or nine. But superpeople didn't need to sleep. They were like robots, computers. They kept on going, operating at peak capacity twenty-four hours every day. Jodi said she was a workaholic, *compulsive* and *fixated*. Naturally Jodi would think it was crazy to work so hard. A little bit of work seemed like an enormous amount to *her*. She was a play-girl.

No two people could have been more un-alike. Yet they were best friends, and they had been for ten years, which just proved how true that old saying really was that op-posites attracted. Even in looks they were al-most opposites. Jodi was tall and athletic, an Amazon, with a fantastic body, perfect di-mensions, rippling muscles, blond hair that was long and thick and gorgeous, blue eyes, an appealing, animated face, dimples, and a perennial smile. She had a perennial suntan, too, since she spent a lot of time at the beach surfing.

Kim was tall, too, but that was the only attribute they had in common. Tall and skinny, straight up and down with no shape whatsoever. No bumps, no curves, no nothing!

Kim had pale skin, pale to the point of translucence. Masses of unruly, thick, overly-curly hair stuck out all over and made her look like the Bride of Frankenstein. Her one arresting feature was her eyes — big, dark brown, soulful eyes that dominated her face.

2

All she saw when she looked at herself in the mirror were masses of hair and enormous sad eyes. Pathetic! She would have loved to trade in the dark hair for blond; the brown eyes for blue, or green like her stepmother, Jan's; and last but definitely not least, the body for one with some of the things girls' bodies were supposed to have, like a chest. Jodi always told her that she was totally gorgeous. Kim knew that Jodi was a little biased — she was her best friend. Of course Kim's boyfriend Brad agreed wholeheartedly with Jodi's assessment of her looks, but he was even more biased than Jodi.

Now Kim was nervous! She kept breaking into a cold sweat. Every time she thought about the afternoon, she got the jitters. After all this time she should have gotten used to this sort of thing, but it just seemed that she never had and probably never would either. She passed the auditorium and saw the notice tacked up on the bulletin board outside the double doors: AUDITIONS, LEAD PARTS, *KISS ME, KATE!*, 3 P.M. As if she needed to be reminded! It was all she had been able to think about for weeks. She had to get that part. She just *had* to. Kim didn't know why she was even worried. Sanders had practically come right out and told her it was hers, hadn't he? She had earned it. She had worked her way up the hard way, from the bottom, spending her first year making sets and costumes, working on lighting, sound, makeup, all those menial jobs.

3

That year, Sanders deigned only to cast her in a walk-on role. No lines. Six months later he gave her the third female lead in Gilbert and Sullivan's *Pirates of Penzance*. Since then she'd had nothing but leads, but this was the part she had been waiting for all her life, the one Sanders had handpicked just for her.

I've got to get that part, she thought grimly as she rushed madly down the stairs, racing the warning bell to English class. *If I don't, I'll just die!*

*T*wo

She bounded across the classroom and collapsed at her desk. She swiveled around in her seat to see if Jodi was in class yet. Jodi was at her desk, draped provocatively across it to flirt with Scott Osborne. To Jodi flirting was second nature, a way of life. She did it without even realizing it. Boys swarmed around her like bees near honey.

Mr. Marsh (alias Marshbanks), their English teacher, came in. Kim waved at Jodi and turned back to face front. Without bothering to take attendance, Marshbanks launched into a lively lecture on Charles Dickens' *David Copperfield*. Normally Kim would have been fascinated. She loved Dickens. But she was too preoccupied to be fascinated by anything today. She doodled on a page in her notebook, designing costumes for Kate. Jodi drew pictures of surfers on hers. She passed Kim a note: *Can you get*

Jan's car tomorrow? Sidney's under the weather again.

Kim turned the note over and scribbled on the back, *I'll check and let you know. Poor Sid,* she thought to herself. Sometimes she forgot he was only a car.

Jan was always accommodating, but Kim didn't like having to borrow her stepmother's car. It meant Jan had to go to work with Kim's father. Then if she wasn't ready to leave work when he was, or if she had to leave early or go somewhere during the day, she wouldn't have transportation.

Under a drawing of herself as Kate in a big-skirted gown with mutton leg sleeves and a plunging neckline, that showed off the cleavage she didn't have, Kim wrote in florid script, KIMBERLY WARRINER STANTON. Warriner was her real mother's maiden name. After the divorce her mother had changed her name back to Warriner. She was Dorothea Elizabeth Warriner again, just as she had been before she married. Kim didn't intend to change her name when she got married. She would remain Kimberly Warriner Stanton, not Kimberly Warriner Stanton Berson or just plain Mrs. Bradley Everett Berson. Who was Mrs. Bradley Everett Berson, anyway? That wasn't *her*. When she was a superstar, she wouldn't bill herself as Mrs. Bradley Everett Berson. She wrote on the next line, KIMBERLY STANTON BERSON. It had a nice ring to it. If she was Kimberly Stanton Berson, she could be Kimberly Stanton, superstar, for professional purposes and Kimberly Berson in private. Kim thought about her professional life. The role of Kate was only a beginning. Should she go over her lines one last time before this afternoon? Brad had said she was overprepared already, and he ought to know. He'd gone through her scene with her at least a dozen times the night before. Was this class ever going to end? Marshbanks had to be the most long-winded human being in history, and he was even *more* so on the subject of Charles Dickens, whom he practically worshipped.

"There will be a quiz on this material tomorrow," he informed the class before leaving the room. "Don't depend on *Cliff's Notes to* get you through it. Take my advice and, if you haven't already, *read the book!*"

"He's dreaming," one of the kids said. "That's got to be the most boring book ever written."

"Deadly," another put in.

"Funny. I loved that book," Kim muttered to Jodi when they were leaving the classroom.

"You would!" Jodi replied.

"You would too if you'd read it."

"Dream on!" Jodi laughed.

"What's with Sidney?" Kim asked.

"I dunno, but I think it's terminal." Jodi treated Scott Osborne to a super-sexy smile. "He's so cute! I never noticed before how cute he is," she said to Kim.

"He's cute, and you happen to be going steady," Kim reminded her.

"The voice of my conscience. Jiminy Cricket," Jodi muttered. Scott caught up with them outside the science lab.

"Hey, Chief baby, got to check something out with you for the paper," he said to Kim.

"Catch me tomorrow," she replied. Debbie Furman waved to her from the lab. "Love your shirt, Kim."

"Thanks! It's my stepmother's." Kim hurried after Jodi. Was Debbie going to audition this afternoon? Who else was going? Probably the same bunch: Debbie, Leslie Chang, Linda Flores, Jean Polanski, Stacy Miller. "It'll be a bona fide miracle if I don't have a complete nervous breakdown by fifth period," Kim said and pretended to tear out her hair.

"You've already got the part, nutcase. Sanders told you so."

"He told me I was just right for it, not that I had it," Kim muttered.

"The world isn't going to end if you don't get to play Kate, is it?"

"As a matter of fact, *yes!*"

"Oh, boy . . . Whoops! Here comes Biggy, and he's wearing his wiggy," Jodi giggled. Mr. Biggar, their beloved principal, bore down on them.

"Young lady, this is the third time this month you've broken the dress rule," he said, staring rather pointedly at Jodi's miniskirt.

"Mr. Biggar, it's too hot for anything

else," Jodi argued, giving his three-piece suit a look that implied it was contagious. Mr. Biggar continued on his way down the hall, shaking his head.

Kim smiled at her friend. "Too hot? Jodi, it's February, not August."

Jodi changed the subject. "You and Brad doing anything special tonight? There's a neat double feature at the Northview Cinema."

"There's a neat double feature at *my* house — homework, then bed."

Jodi sighed. "You're so predictable! Work, work, work. Work and worry. Worry and work. Depressing lifestyle. You used to be an okay kid before you turned into a raving workaholic, you know it? I have a hot flash for you, kiddo. There's more to life than working and worrying. For instance, ever hear of fun, F.U.N.? It's got the two W's beat by miles. Try it sometime. You may never go back to W and W again."

"Weekends are for F.U.N.; weeknights for W.O.R.K. *You* ought to try it. You might wind up with a halfway decent report card. How does it feel to be on the receiving end for once, Adams?" Kim laughed when Jodi looked aggrieved. "You can dish it out, but you can't take it."

"That goes without saying," Jodi murmured.

Tony sauntered down the corridor toward them, Mr. Movie Star in his fifties getup with his hair slicked back on the sides and puffed up on top in a pompadour. He was Jodi's latest boyfriend. He probably wouldn't be her boyfriend for long. She was notoriously fickle. That was another thing she and Kim didn't have in common. Kim had been going steady with Brad for two years. Jodi changed boyfriends as easily as she changed clothes. Tony grabbed her and kissed her in the corridor in front of everybody, a whole bunch of kids and a few of the teachers. Jodi wasn't in the least embarrassed. She didn't have a self-conscious bone in her body. Nothing bothered her, but Kim would have died on the spot if Brad had done a thing like that. He never would have, of course, knowing how she felt.

Kim hurried to the cafeteria. She was worried about Margie Kaplow's speech. It could wind up losing the team the state finals. After what Kim had gone through to get them to third place — all the way up from fifteenth — she wasn't about to let that happen.

Margie was concentrating on her lunch.

"Let's get to work," Kim said and sat down at the table opposite her.

"When I'm done eating," Margie replied, toying with a forkful of chicken a la king. Kim decided to get yogurt and a piece of fruit. Just then Ann Rosen and Mary Mackay walked by. Mary looked at Kim and said, "Well, why worry about the audition, Ann? Miss Perfect here is Sanders' pet."

Kim stammered, "Until the list goes up, no

one's sure about anything." She looked back at Margie. Ann and Mary moved on. Kim hated herself for letting Mary intimidate her, but she was always intimidated by people whom she knew didn't like her, and Mary loathed her. Kim had no idea why. They didn't even really know one another. But ever since Mary came to Montebello the beginning of last year, she had made it more than obvious how she felt.

"She must have read that book, *How to Win Friends and Influence People*," Margie said when Mary and Ann walked away.

"She's gone now. Let's get to work, okay?" Kim said abruptly.

Margie clinked her spoon against the inside of her dessert dish. "Um, well, I . . . that is . . . see, it's like . . ."

"You did the outline, didn't you, Margie?"

"Uh, well, actually, no. Look, I'm really sorry. I know I should have, but my sister happens to be getting married in a couple of weeks, and it's pretty frantic at my house. I mean, we're having the wedding at home, and there's so much to do, and, well, with the SATs coming up, and today's auditions, I just couldn't get to it."

Kim studied the cover of her math book. She wanted to say, "If you weren't prepared, why didn't you tell me so I wouldn't waste my time." She didn't. One of her ongoing problems was her reluctance to confront difficult or unpleasant situations. *Naughty, naughty! You're not being awfully assertive,*

Stanton. Or awfully honest either. Why not tell the girl what's on your mind? You'll feel a lot better if you do.

"I feel like a rat. I mean it," Margie went on.

"It's okay. Really," Kim murmured, her eyes riveted on her textbook.

"I'll do it over the weekend, I promise. We can work on it Monday," Margie vowed. Kim nodded mutely. Monday. Always one of her more frantic days, and since Wednesday was the day the newspaper had to go to the printer's, this Monday would be even more frantic than most. Well, she'd have to fit this in. What could she do? They weren't about to lose those finals if she could help it. She gathered her things and stood up.

"See you Monday, Margie."

"Great! I'll have it all done by then. Thanks a lot, Kim. You're a doll," Margie called after her.

If she had ever had an appetite, it was gone now. She bought herself a container of milk and an apple at the snack dispenser. The apple was dry and woody, so she threw it away and just drank the milk.

Jodi would have lectured her about the episode with Margie. "So what if the debating team loses the finals? That's not your personal failure. You're not the whole team. Just the captain." Why did Jodi think it was so wrong to want to win? Why be a loser when there was the potential to be a winner? Why be second best?

"Anything worth doing is worth doing right." That was one of her father's credos. "If you aren't willing to extend yourself and give it your all, then don't bother to do it in the first place." She could just hear him. Well, it was easier for him than her. He was a born overachiever and excelled at everything he did. If he knew he couldn't excel at it, he didn't do it.

"He expects himself to be perfect, and he expects you to be too," Jodi was always saying. But who could be perfect? It was humanly impossible. Her nickname was a joke, and not a funny one. Miss Perfect. People thought she was perfect, but what did they know about her? Nothing! Only she knew the real Kim Stanton, the one she was inside, and that Kim was far from perfect.

Three

On her way to psych, Kim ran into Mr. Sanders. Sheldon Sanders was enormous, nearly six-three, built like a linebacker for the L.A. Rams. He had curly red hair and a red beard to match, and while he looked like an outdoorsman, he was really an intellectual. Whenever Kim saw him, he had his nose in a book. Acting, books, and music. Those were the only three things he cared about. Acting, and the theater in general, came first. He ate, breathed, and slept it. It was his life, which was too bad since at this point he could only experience it secondhand. He had been an actor when he was younger, but he had had to give it up because he had a family to support and couldn't earn a living acting. It was a familiar story, one she knew a little bit about. Her father had gone through the same thing when *he* was young. Mr. Sanders had become a teacher of actors instead of an actor. Kim often wondered if he was frustrated and bitter about that.

He was a first-rate teacher. He knew talent when he saw it, and he knew how to bring it out, develop it, and refine it. He had turned out quite a few people over the years who had gone on, after graduating Montebello High, to become successful professional actors. Sanders liked to take credit for having discovered them.

He had been the one who had first recognized Kim's talent and had talked her into joining the Thespians her first year at Montebello. It had been a terrible year in her life: she still hadn't gotten used to missing her mother, and her father was going to remarry. The drama club had given her an outlet for her emotions. It was something to be involved in, and concentrate her energies on, other than simply being miserable. It had been like therapy in a way, and she had always been grateful to Mr. Sanders for talking her into theater. He'd let her know she *had* talent, and that her dream of being an actress wasn't just a dream. He smiled at her now.

"Auditioning this afternoon?" he asked, knowing that she was.

"Hyperventilating," she laughed ruefully, falling into step with him. "After all the auditions I've lived through, wouldn't you think I'd be used to them by now? I'm so nervous!"

"Being nervous keeps your energy level up," he pointed out.

"Mr. Sanders, after knowing me this long, you ought to know my energy level's *always* up. I'm hyper."

"Also exhausted," he added, studying her face intensely.

She blushed and stammered, "It's the lights. They make everybody look kind of green around the gills."

"Is that the latest *un*-hairstyle?" he asked, looking at her unruly mane.

"Um, not really. More like I just haven't had time to get it cut."

"I like it. It suits you; accentuates your features and those big, beautiful eyes."

Her face was burning. She didn't know where to look. Or what to say. So she muttered, "I'll be late," and took off, feeling inadequate as usual.

All the students adored Sanders. He was somewhat of a cult hero around Montebello High. He didn't get along all that well with the staff, especially the administrative staff, but there wasn't a student in the school who didn't worship him. He just wasn't like the other teachers. He even dressed like one of the students, usually in jeans, a sport shirt, a sweatshirt or sweater, and always tennis shoes or sandals. Kim didn't think he even owned anything else. In ninth grade she had had a mad crush on him. Of course she had been young then. She knew he took a very special interest in her, in her work and her

16

future. If there was such a thing as a teacher's pet, she was his. Everyone knew it. A lot of the kids resented it. She was embarrassed by it when it exhibited itself in front of other people, but secretly she loved the fact that he thought so highly of her, or rather of her abilities, and that he set her above all the others.

She was early for psych. Ms. Horikawa was at the back of the classroom struggling to thread a spool of film onto a projector. Kim went to help her. Her father was a film editor, so she knew how to do things like that.

Kim was glad they were seeing a film today. She certainly wasn't in the mood for a normal class. She'd never be able to concentrate in her current mental state. The film was an enactment of an actual case study taken from a psychiatrist's files, the case of a sixteen-year-old girl who had tried to commit suicide, ostensibly because she hadn't gotten invited to her senior prom. Three minutes into the film Kim knew the prom wasn't really the reason. The girl had parents who were always pushing her to achieve, criticizing her if she didn't live up to their expectations, and their expectations were so high that they were almost impossible to live up to, which meant the girl went through life failing constantly or thinking she did. The film ended on a somewhat positive note, with the girl and her parents going to a psychiatrist for professional help, beginning to get in touch with their problems.

Kim had the impression that the girl realized there *was* hope for the future and wouldn't attempt suicide again.

"I always *did* love happy endings," Jodi said when they were leaving the classroom. "That movie was a downer!"

"That's reality," Kim told her. "It's not always happy, like in old movies. Real life's a kick in the head sometimes."

"Tell me about it. Listen, I don't blame her for trying to kill herself. I would, too, if I had parents like that," Jodi went on.

Debbie Furman heard her and said, "If I didn't get invited to my senior prom, I'd kill myself."

"Well, let's just hope you get invited then," Jodi said, looking at Kim.

"Do you believe her?" Kim said when they were walking away. Kim glanced at Jodi, who was looking at her very oddly. "Why are you looking at me like that? You think *I'm* like the girl in the movie, don't you?" she declared defensively.

Jodi turned around to admire Rob Cordier in his T-shirt and skintight jeans. "What's with you lately? I swear, you're getting paranoid. Who said anything about *you*? You're a perfectionist, but only a semi-neurotic one. I doubt if you'd run right out and kill yourself the first time you didn't get straight A's or get invited to a school dance. Lock yourself in your closet for a week maybe, but kill yourself? No way!"

"Very funny, Adams! You *do* think I'm like that girl."

Jodi stopped and stood with her hands on her hips frowning at her. "Know what I think? You're losing your grip, kiddo. It's true. All this work, rushing around, trying to do so many things, never able to keep up with it all. It's making you cuckoo."

Ben Hernandez strolled by, flexed his muscles at Jodi, and drawled, "Put your eyes back in your head, Adams. Yeah, I know. I'm irresistible. A shame you're going steady."

"Have you noticed he's getting better looking?" Jodi whispered to Kim. "I love his new hairstyle. Makes him look like James Dean."

Kim shook her head. "Every boy looks like James Dean to you."

"James Dean is gorgeous, the most gorgeous man ever. He just happens to be my favorite actor in the world," Jodi declared.

"Unfortunately he also happens to be dead, so the chances of the two of you getting together aren't too terrific." Kim fished in her satchel for her change purse and got out a coin for the pay phone. She had a couple of minutes before next period. Just enough time for a quick call to Brad. He would be at home between classes. Brad was eighteen, two years older than Kim, and in his first year at UCLA.

Kim hurried to the phone booth outside the boys' gym, dropped the coin in the slot, and dialed his number. "It's me, your emotionally distraught girlfriend. Help! I'm in need of moral support," she said when Brad came on the line.

"How do you feel?"

"Frantic, thank you," Kim said, trying to sound breezy.

"Naturally. If you ever took an audition in stride, I'd faint from the shock. Look, you're getting yourself all upset over nothing. You've got the part already. Sanders told you, didn't he? You *are* Kate, my bonny Kate, Kate the Curse. Don't cut your hair. Kate had long hair," Brad finished.

"How do you know?"

"I know everything, don't I?" he asked.

"Right. I forgot. Okay, no haircut. I wish this was over with. And I wish you were here to give me moral support. And I wish I were doing the scene with you instead of Ben Hernandez. He's such a geek!"

"Pretend he's me," Brad advised. "Listen, we'll celebrate tonight. I'm going to get totally carried away and spring for Chinese food. And if that doesn't prove my undying adoration, I don't know what *does*."

She laughed and said, "Moo Shu Pork?"

"Absolutely!"

Kim smiled. "Mmm, tempting, but that's one of the reasons I called you now instead of when I get home. I have to cancel tonight, Brad. I can't go. I've got tons of work to do, more than I thought, and I haven't been getting nearly enough sleep lately. I've got to catch up, or I'll conk out. Lately I feel like a zombie. You won't like having a zombie for a girlfriend."

"Oh, I don't know. It might be a change of pace. Listen, we'll make it an early evening, okay?" There was a tone in Brad's voice that Kim hadn't heard before.

Kim answered, "I don't think so. Honestly, I think I'd better just stay in, get my homework done early, and sack out. If I could get one good night's sleep, like nine or ten hours, I'd feel better, I just know it."

"Good thing I'm super-confident, or I'd think you didn't love me anymore, the way you keep breaking dates with me," he said, sounding disappointed. It made her feel guilty. "Do you have any idea how many nights in a row we haven't seen each other? I forgot what you look like," he went on.

"Just look at my picture. Look, we'll make up for it this weekend," she said a little anxiously. Did he think she liked staying home, slaving over her homework, when she could be out enjoying herself with him? Did he think it was easy for her?

"Okay, Sleeping Beauty, but you'll be sorry. Right after I hang up this phone, I'm going to go out and kill myself." He sounded hesitant to end the conversation.

"There's a lot of that going around today. Must be the planets. Don't do anything messy, okay?" Kim teased.

"How about if I leap off a tall building?"

"There aren't any tall buildings in the area," she reminded him.

"I could drown myself, only we just drained the pool," he murmured. "Good thing I'm basically a loner, or I might consider finding somebody else to spend those long, lonely evenings with when you're communing with your textbooks."

"Do it, and you won't have to kill yourself. I'll do it for you!"

"You jealous? A good sign! Reassuring. Listen, don't worry. The part's yours. Go out there and slay 'em, baby. Knock their socks off." He made a kissing noise and hung up. She pushed open the door of the phone booth feeling a little let down. She had called him because she had needed a lift, some tender loving care and moral support, but he had laid a guilt trip on her instead. She knew he hadn't meant to, but still it was a guilt trip. Did she have a choice about breaking those dates? What was she supposed to do, get rid of all her responsibilities and commitments, spend all her time going out and having fun? Even if she wanted to, she couldn't. It wasn't her style. She never took on a responsibility, then dispensed with it. She didn't take one on unless she knew she would be willing to do her utmost to fulfill it to the best of her ability. Why didn't Brad understand that?

F*our*

Kim sat in the center-aisle seat, fifth row, chewing her fingernails. It was her lucky seat, the one she always sat in when she was auditioning. Not that she was superstitious or anything, but if she'd had a rabbit's foot, she would have been hanging onto it for dear life. Dumb! Luck had nothing to do with this. Sanders was making the final decision, and he wanted her to play Kate, so what was she getting herself into a hysterical state about?

"I came to give you moral support," Jodi said, slipping into the seat next to her.

Kim grabbed her hand and held on tight. "Adams, you always come through!"

"Naturally. Isn't that what best friends are supposed to do?"

"Yeah, but not too many of them do it. God, I'm a mess! I swear, Jodi, being an actress is all I've ever wanted in life, but if

I'm going to have to go through this every-time I have to try out for a part, maybe I ought to think about going into some other line of work."

"Like what?"

"Ditch digging maybe? I could be a writer like my mother, only I don't think I'm smart enough," Kim mused. Jodi burst out laughing. Obviously she thought that was incredibly amusing. "Just because someone's a hard worker doesn't mean they're innately smart," Kim informed her. "It works the other way around, too. Just because someone doesn't get top grades doesn't mean they're *not*. Take you, for example. You happen to be extremely intelligent, but you don't extend yourself or do any work, so it doesn't show up in your schoolwork."

Mr. Sanders came in, walked up the center aisle to the front of the auditorium, and said, "Hey, people, I know you're all wondering why I asked you here today." Naturally everybody broke up. "So, listen, who wants to go first?" he said, rubbing his hands together. He looked around to see if anyone raised his, or her, hand. Tentatively Stacy Miller put up hers. "Stacy, my sweet, you're on!" he declared and, with a flourish, helped her out of her seat, down the aisle, and up onto the stage. Kim mentally appraised Stacy's tryout, and the tryout of each actress who followed her. Stacy was a windup doll, and she couldn't carry a tune to save herself. Jean Polanski tried out next. Jean *had* talent.

Unfortunately she didn't think so. She was always putting herself down, telling everybody how untalented she was. Debbie Furman could sing a little, but she couldn't act her way out of a paper bag. After Debbie came Margie. She had a certain quality — appealing, very dynamic — and she moved well. She could play comedy roles very well. Kim had a feeling she would probably get the part of Bianca. Next came Linda Flores, who looked like one of those pretty porcelain dolls you saw in antique shops. She *looked* like Kate, but she couldn't sing or act.

"I don't know why any of them bother to audition. They look pretty bad next to *you*," Jodi whispered. Kim's turn was next. She rearranged her features into a smile, her public smile, the one she reserved for these occasions. She stood up and, giving Jodi's hand a squeeze, made her way to the aisle, then strode purposely down it to the stage, head high. She looked like the world's most self-assured, self-confident, poised young woman. She took her place center stage. Sanders struck a chord on the piano. She began to sing her solo from Act Two.

"I hate men!
I can't abide them even now and then."

She could tell she was doing well. She projected her voice all the way up to the second balcony, focusing on a spot somewhere halfway to the back of the auditorium. Breathing was the key to good delivery. Her vocal coach had taught her that. She had a trained voice and had been taking acting and ballet lessons for years, ever since she was little. She knew it gave her an edge over the others. She finished the song and heard Jodi give out with one of her infamous whistles, usually reserved for baseball stadiums and fight arenas. But that was Jodi, enthusiastic right down to her toes. Ben Hernandez came onstage, and they ran through the scene they had prepared, the one in which Ben, as Petruchio, took her over his knee and spanked her. Ben seemed to be putting a whole lot more enthusiasm into it than he had when they had rehearsed it.

"Try doing that on opening night, you'll never make the second performance, buster!" she growled at him when they were leaving the stage. He swept off an imaginary hat, made a low bow, and stepped aside so she could precede him. On the way down the steps, she gave him a swift poke in the ribs with her elbow.

"*Oof!*" He staggered into the wings, then emerged, clutching his belly, and did a death scene. Everybody broke up. Kim swept up the aisle. She heard Mary Mackay say, "Why does Sanders bother to hold auditions? We all know he's giving her the part."

"You were unreal!" Jodi whispered when she collapsed into her seat.

"You're partial," Kim gasped, clutching her hand so hard she let out a yelp. "God, I'm shaking like a leaf. I think I'm going to throw up, I mean it."

"No, you're not!" Jodi admonished.

Three boys tried out for Petruchio: Ben, Scott, and B. J. Burnside. Seven others auditioned for the other male parts. When Kim thought she couldn't stand the suspense another second, Sanders made an announcement.

"Thank you all for your time. You were splendid." He cleared his throat and then continued. "The names of the leads will be posted on the bulletin board outside the auditorium first thing Monday morning." His words were met with a shocked silence. Looking uncomfortable, Sanders turned and strode quickly offstage. This wasn't the way he usually did it. He always told them right away. Why was he making them go through three days before they found out? Talk about torture! Having been an actor himself once, he ought to know better.

"You dirty rat!" Ben said, imitating James Cagney, when Sanders had left the auditorium. "I'll get you for this."

"I don't believe this is happening," Kim said to Jodi.

"Is he putting us on?" she heard Margie say.

"I think he means it," Ann Rosen grumbled.

"Maybe he wants to make it look as though he took time to decide," Mary Mackay said, looking straight at Kim, "but we all know who he's giving the part of Kate to, don't we, kiddies? None other than Miss Perfect herself!"

*F*ive

"Why'd he *do* that?" Jodi asked, slipping in behind the wheel of her decrepit old Mustang convertible. She pumped the gas pedal a few times for insurance, then turned the ignition on. The engine turned over, coughed, then died. Jodi patted the dashboard and said sweetly, "Be nice, Sidney, or Mama will have to take you to the junkyard and tell the bad man there to dismantle you and sell you for scrap. You won't like being dismantled, Sidney. It hurts!" She said to Kim, "If *he* goes, that's the end of *me*. Without wheels I might as well become a hermit, go into seclusion, retire from the human race. How can you get around in this godforsaken place without wheels? Good Sidney. Nice Sidney. Be a good boy . . . *puleeze*?" she cooed and, as though it were responding to her, the car started. Kim sat there feeling mildly nauseated. Her head hurt, a dull thud behind her eyes. *Why did he do that?* she kept asking herself. *Why?*

"Would Jan be hysterical if you had to borrow her car more often?" Jodi asked as she pulled out of the parking space.

"Not hysterical, but it sure would inconvenience her. I hate having to borrow it as it is. Wish I could get a part-time job. Then maybe I could save up for a car of my own," Kim replied distractedly, thinking about Sanders and the weekend ahead.

"That'll be the day, when your father lets you work. If you worked, you wouldn't be able to devote as much time to your schoolwork. And if you couldn't devote as much time to your schoolwork, you might not get all A's. And if you didn't get all A's — I mean if you happened to get one little B on your report card or something — well, that would be disastrous, wouldn't it? You may not be suicidal, kiddo, but you *are* like that girl in the flick, at least in that way."

"Jodi, don't start in on me again," Kim warned, "and don't you dare say anything derogatory about my father either. It's just not right the way you put him down all the time. How would you like it if I said derogatory things about *your* father?"

"Oops! Sorry. I forget you're not supposed to say anything derogatory about the King." Jodi pretended to zip her mouth closed.

Kim thought it was time to change the subject.

"I heard from my mother. She called and

offered to send me money to help me toward my own car," she remarked, looking out the window.

"She did? Yee-gads! When are you going to get it?" Jodi squealed excitedly.

"I might not. I feel funny taking money from her," Kim replied slowly.

"Why? She's your mother. Besides, if you refuse, you're liable to make her feel rejected, and you wouldn't want *that*."

Kim burst out laughing. "Where did you get *that*, Sigmund Freud?"

"In our psych textbook."

"You mean you actually opened it and read it? A miracle!" Kim laughed at her friend, relaxing a little.

Sidney picked that moment to rebel. He stalled at a stop sign. Jodi coerced and cajoled him into action again. She said, "I don't know how long he'll last. Not long, the rate he's going. If you got a car, we'd be okay. Otherwise we're both going to end up recluses. You don't want to be a recluse, do you? Oops! I forgot. You're one already."

"Jodi . . ."

"Okay, okay, I'll shut up, but I worry about you. You're so . . ."

"Fixated?" Kim finished for her.

"Yeah, right. Look, you're only young once. Clichéd, but true. So why blow it? You won't get another time 'round if you *do*. Someday, when you're old, sitting in a rocker, rocking your declining years away, you'll look back on all this and say, 'Ah, the dear, dead days of my lost youth. I blew them. Why didn't I go out and have a ball instead of working my butt off?' "

"That's not what I'll say at all," Kim laughed. "I'll be this venerated, revered actress, a Hollywood institution, like Katharine Hepburn, only greater. And I'll sit in that rocker, and I'll say to myself, 'Ah, the dear, dead days of my lost youth. I don't regret one moment of them. What I did back then got me where I am today.' "

"Famous last words! You should live so long," Jodi said, pulling into Kim's driveway. She kept the motor running just to be on the safe side. Kim climbed out of the car.

"If you don't hear from me, just assume I've got the car tomorrow. Pick you up at the usual time," she said, and giving Sidney a pat for luck, started up the front path to the house. Jodi took off up Cypress Street in a cloud of smoke. Kim got out her house key. Three days to get through before she found out. *How could Sanders do it, especially when he knows damned well how it feels to be on the receiving end?* The audition had been stressful enough, to say nothing of the anxiety leading up to it. He could have told them right away as he usually did, and it would all be over now. This only prolonged it. Three more days . . .

Kim let herself into the house. It was more like a stable converted into a house. Ten years ago it *had* been the stable on a big estate. Then the estate had been sold, the property divided into parcels, one of which had the stable on it. Kim's father had come along, fallen in love with the stable on sight, and hocked his soul to buy it. He'd then spent years fixing it up, turning it into the most beautiful house in the world in Kim's opinion.

Carpentry was Sam Stanton's hobby. At least he called it a hobby. He could have been a master carpenter. He could build a piece of furniture from scratch and make it look exactly like a priceless antique. He was a perfectionist. He did everything to perfection. He was always saying that anything that was worth doing was worth doing right. Kim's problem was that he did everything right, and it all came so easily to him. That was the one way they weren't alike. She was good at everything, too, but for her it was hard work.

Kim's mother had hated the house and resented all the time, effort, and money he had put into it. It was just one of a host of things her parents *didn't* agree on. Come to think of it, Kim couldn't think of one thing they *did* agree on. Talk about bad marriages! Theirs could have won first prize in the Worst Marriages in America Contest, which made it just as well that they had finally decided to end it. When the decision had been made, and her mother had left, Kim had actually felt relieved. It had made her feel guilty, but she hadn't been able to help it. For the first time in her life there was peace in the house. No more fighting. She hated when anyone fought. It made her so uptight and apprehensive. The pain of missing her mother, terrible at first, had lessened over the years.

She dumped her things on the antique hat stand in the entry and was on her way into the kitchen when she heard a familiar sound, Brad's VW cranking noisily up the driveway. She flung open the kitchen door and yelled to him, "What are *you* doing here? Nice you're still alive. When are you going to do it, by the way?"

"Do what?" he asked, coming to kiss her.

"Kill yourself. You said you were going to."

"I'm on my way to find a tall building at this very moment. How come you're not upstairs communing with Pythagoras?"

"I just got home."

"I always *did* have great timing!" he said proudly.

"This is true."

"I just stopped by to look at you. See, I haven't seen you for so long, I forgot what you looked like. Just wanted to refresh my memory. You're pretty, you know it? Mind if I stay a couple of minutes so I can look at you some more?" he finished, out of breath.

"Help yourself, but then you've got to go. Homework, remember?" Kim tried to sound flip, but she was serious.

"You're not going to offer me something to eat? Here I am, about to succumb, mere minutes away from utter starvation. You have a kitchen literally loaded with food, and you don't offer me a single bite. Heartless creature!"

"Have a yogurt," she said, going to get two out of the refrigerator. Before she could close the door, he grabbed an apple, an orange, and a package of Monterey Jack cheese. He went to get a box of crackers from the pantry and a knife and spoon from the drawer and sat down at the table.

Kim didn't say so, but she was glad he had come. Being with him lifted her spirits, and right now they were badly in need of bolstering. "Just make yourself at home," she said, watching him devour the food.

"Thanks. I *will*," he replied, cutting the apple into slices. "This has got to be the neatest kitchen in the history of kitchens. Jan ought to get it into one of those home-decorating magazines. I mean it."

The kitchen was her father's handiwork. He had not only designed it, but built it himself, every square inch of it; he even laid the quarry-tile floor, hung the solid oak cabinets, put in the appliances and the windows. A real old-fashioned country kitchen was one of his dreams. He had always wanted one, and now he had it. Jan loved plants, and the room was filled with them. She had a green thumb.

Kim watched Brad eat. "You're disgusting! Honestly, I don't know what I see in you," she said. He wasn't handsome. He wasn't tall. In fact, when she was wearing heels, they were the same height. He wasn't a jock or built like one with rippling muscles. Despite the fact that he wasn't all those things, he was very appealing, irresistible, in fact, at least to *her*. What was it? His blond hair? It *was* beautiful — curly and glossy, slightly on the long side. He was kind of vain about it. He *did* have the prettiest dark blue eyes, or rather they were dark blue right now. They changed color depending on what he wore. His features were uneven: a slightly crooked nose, a too-wide mouth, and ears that stuck out. Jodi said he looked like a leprechaun. Kim tried to imagine what he would look like when he got older. Certainly not one of those nondescript middle-aged men who kind of disappeared into a crowd, the type you never looked at twice. She thought he would probably improve with age. Anyway, she hoped so. If they had children, she hoped they would all look like him, not her.

"What are you thinking about?" he asked.

"You."

."No wonder you're smiling. Why am I so hungry all the time? Do you think I have a tapeworm?"

"You're a growing boy, that's all."

"Growing at eighteen? I doubt it. Hey, if you wanted tall, dark, and handsome, sorry. You're out of luck."

"You mean you're not? Good heavens, and all this time I thought you were Rock Hudson!"

"Are you going to tell me about the audition, or am I going to sit here having palpitations all afternoon?" he asked, then devoured a banana in two gulps. "I can't believe I've been here all this time, nearly ten minutes, and you haven't uttered a syllable about it. What d'you think I came for, your Monterey Jack cheese and yogurt?"

"There's good news, and there's bad news," she began, feeling the apprehension come back to plague her.

"Gimme the good news first."

"I was terrific."

"That's not news. So?"

"So, the bad news. Sanders isn't going to reveal the identity of the leading players until Monday morning!" she announced in a terribly British, matronly voice. Brad put down an apple.

"I don't believe him! What's with this guy? How callous and insensitive! He's unfeeling! He's a teacher, supposedly tuned into how kids feel about things. Yet he goes out of his way to zap you with *this*. All I can say is the man's lost *my* respect."

Kim tried to rationalize it. "He's just trying to protect himself. He's already made up his mind, but he doesn't want anyone to know it because they might think he's playing favorites, picking me."

"Logical," he mused, chomping on a cracker. "But it doesn't sound like Sanders. Since when does he knuckle under to the administration, especially Biggy?"

"He needs this job, Brad."

"Yeah, well, maybe you're right."

"I probably *am*. Maybe he'll go all the way and protect himself by giving the part to someone else."

"Not a chance! No one else can play it."

"Yes, but it's a high school play, not Broadway. So, who's going to care one way or the other?"

"Plenty of people. It's not just any high school. It's Montebello High, and Montebello High has a reputation, remember? Sanders is always bragging about all the people who've gone from there to the big time. How about all those big deal Hollywood directors and producers who come to see the productions looking for new talent? What about that guy last year, your father's friend? He wasn't exactly there for his health either," Brad reminded her. She had to admit he was right. That guy last year had turned out to be a big Hollywood agent, and he had come backstage to congratulate her. He'd told her that anytime she was ready to think about starting a professional career as an actress, he would be happy to represent her.

"I'm still hungry," Brad said and went to look in the fridge. He came back with a casserole of leftover spaghetti and meatballs and started to devour it. "Know what Brett did the other day? Went to Chippendale's and applied for a job as a singing waiter."

"A singing waiter? Uh, that's not what I hear the waiters do at Chippendale's."

"I always wanted an exotic dancer for a brother," Brad laughed, shaking his head.

"The idiot tried to con me into going over there and filling out an application, too. He says the pay is great — with a lot of tips."

"Mmm, right. You *do*. The ladies throw money at you for taking your clothes off. I can just see you scrambling around the stage in your BVD's, picking up dimes and quarters and tucking them in your, um, *whatevers*. Actually, you'd be terrific as an exotic dancer, only maybe you wouldn't like it all that much being a sex symbol," Kim said.

"I could live with it if the money was good. Would you come and see me perform?" he asked innocently and popped a meatball in his mouth.

"Only if you promise to take it all off."

"You're on!" he laughed and did a couple of bumps and grinds for her entertainment. He started to tell her about his acting class at UCLA. The class was doing *A Streetcar Named Desire*, in which he was playing Stanley Kowalski. Some girl in his class named Sherry was playing Stanley's wife, Stella.

"What's she look like?" Kim asked.

"You jealous or something?"

"No. Just curious," Kim answered.

"Pretty. Blond hair, green eyes. Great bod. Wears too much makeup, though," Brad said, wiping his hands on a napkin.

"Do you get to kiss her?"

"No. Just grab her a lot." He grinned at Kim.

"Is she a good actress?" Kim had to know.

"Not in your league."

"Well, that's something, anyway."

He pulled her into his arms and kissed her. They stood there kissing for quite a while, until she happened to think about the time. "You've got to go. You know what? Kissing can be very time-consuming."

"One more kiss," he pleaded.

"Brad, you're doing it again."

"Doing what?"

"You know. Taking advantage of me."

He leered at her, twirled the ends of an imaginary moustache, and began to creep stealthily around the kitchen doing one of those dastardly villains from the old silent movies. "One last kiss, me pretty, or I'll foreclose on your dear papa's mortgage, and he'll lose his proverbial shoit!" He lunged at her, grabbed her, bent her over backwards, in a kiss straight out of a 1920's movie.

"Next think you know I'll be in the hospital in traction with a slipped disc," she said, struggling to get free.

"Heh, heh, heh! I'll have my way with you, me pretty, or my name isn't Mervyn Magruder, Esk!"

"Mervyn Magruder, Esk?" she choked, convulsed with laughter. A dozen kisses, and fifteen minutes later, she finally managed to coerce him into leaving. On the way down the driveway to his car, he did Hamlet's soliloquy at the top of his lungs in a heavy Russian accent. "I love you, Bradley Everett!" she called after him as he took off down the front walk.

Six

Jan had left a note on her desk, propped up against the antique inkwell. *Hope all went well. Wish I could have been there. Love you, Jan.*

It was typical of her to remember, Kim thought. With all she had on her mind, it was a wonder she *had*. Her publicity job was so incredibly demanding, yet she was involved in so many other things, too. Kim had lucked out getting her for a stepmother. She was caring and understanding and *fun*. Of course Jan wasn't anywhere near as old as most of Kim's friends' mothers. She was only ten years older than Kim, more like a friend than a mother.

Kim had been upset when her father announced he was going to remarry. After he and her mother divorced, he had vowed he never would. The second time around he had gone out of his way to pick someone just the opposite from her mother. Some people had been shocked when that someone turned out to be twenty-four years old, fifteen years younger than him, but Kim didn't think that age mattered all that much. If two people loved each other, got along, and had things in common, what did it matter? Besides, her mother and father were exactly the same age, and they had been totally incompatible.

Kim had always been closer to her father than to her mother. Actually she had been inordinately close to her father and not close at all to her mother.

She had a feeling they could have been a lot closer now; that is, if her mother hadn't lived so far away. It was a little hard to be on intimate terms with someone when there were three thousand miles separating you. Her mother lived in New York — in Greenwich Village. She was a writer, and she had just recently sold her first novel to a big New York publisher. It was cause for celebration, and naturally her mother was jubilant. Kim had a little difficulty picturing her mother jubilant, or even moderately content, or much of anything except uncommunicative and depressed.

Maybe that wasn't fair. After all, she had been younger when they were all still together. Maybe her judgment hadn't been as well developed as it was now. She could have been seeing things from a biased viewpoint. She *could* have, but Kim didn't think so. It had been four-and-a-half years since her parents' divorce, and at this point she could hardly remember what her mother had been like back then. Whatever her mother had been like then, she was different now. She had changed drastically. Not a little at a time. Almost all at once the minute she'd walked out the door. It was as though she had been in prison, then suddenly liberated, which is probably exactly the way it had felt to *her*. Before she left, she had been one person. Now she was another. Kim still couldn't get used to it.

All her life people had been telling her how like her father she was. Everyone said they were two peas in a pod. They had everything in common. They looked alike, thought alike, liked all the same things, and had the same interests and talents. It was a little disconcerting sometimes being so precisely like another person, especially when the other person was male and forty-one years old, and you were female and sixteen.

Kim's father had started out wanting to be an actor, too, but he had had to give up acting, for the same reason Mr. Sanders had, because he had a family to support. He liked to imagine that he would have been a big success if reality hadn't come along and circumvented his plans for the future. But instead of becoming an actor, he had become a film editor, one of the best in the business: he was always in demand at all the major film studios. He and Jan had met working on a film: she had arranged the publicity; he had done the editing.

Kim didn't think her father was bitter about having to give up acting. He'd found something else he liked to do as much. Well, *almost* as much. Film editing was in the same industry and almost as creative. As a parent, he really took his responsibilities to heart. Kim knew that some parents, especially single ones, could get so involved trying to work out their own problems, they forget that their kids have problems, too. Her father had always put her needs and her welfare before everything.

After her mother left, he could have gone out, like some men, and done the whole swinging-single scene, but he had stayed home and done the parental one instead. Her mother had wanted Kim to come and live with her, but he had fought it, threatening to take her to court. Her mother had acquiesced rather than put Kim in that position. Kim suspected that being a single parent would have been tough for anyone. But Sam was a natural-born parent. He had taken on the responsibilities not just willingly, but eagerly, and had made a lot of personal sacrifices to raise Kim.

Well, I'll repay him someday, she thought, rummaging in her satchel for her assignment book. He had such high hopes for her, and she was determined to make sure he would see them fulfilled. After all he had done for her, that was the least she could do for him.

She got out her math book. She always got

the math out of the way first, because it was
the hardest. She was just getting into her
English assignment when she heard Jan come
in downstairs. The first thing Jan did was
come up to ask how the audition went.

"Okay, but we won't know who's getting
the parts 'til Monday morning," Kim said,
getting up and following her down the hall
to the master bedroom. She flopped down on
the chaise lounge.

"How come?" Jan asked, peeling off her
clothes.

"I don't know. Ask Sanders. Anyway, no
biggy. I can handle it," she said, mentally
adding, *Liar*!

Jan shrugged out of her silk skirt. "You
shouldn't have to. I thought he was going to
tell you today. Really! What a thoughtless,
inconsiderate thing to do."

"I'll tell him you said so," Kim said with a
grin. She propped her feet on the carved
wooden frame of the chaise. How she adored
this room! It was straight out of a home-
decorating magazine, almost too pretty to use.
Jan had redecorated it after she and Kim's
father got married. Pink roses bloomed on a
white background on the wallpaper. There
was matching fabric on the bedspread, the
heavy tie-back drapes, and even the uphol-
stery on the chaise. The room was like one big
rose garden. Kim expected to hear birds singing and a breeze sighing through the trees.
Kim had liked the room so much that, when
it came time to redecorate her own room, she

asked Jan to do it in the same overall style. Instead of pink roses in bloom on the wallpaper and matching fabric, her room had pink rosebuds *about* to bloom; and instead of heavy, ornate Victorian furniture, hers was white rattan.

"What are you wearing tonight?" Kim asked when Jan came out of the bathroom.

"You're asking *me*? I haven't got a thing," Jan groaned and started dragging things out of her closet, piling them up on the bed.

"Really! It's so unfair, my boss's making me attend these things. *I'm* not the head of the department. *He* is. Why doesn't *he* go and let me stay home where I belong?" She held up a long dress, dove gray silk crepe with a high neck and long ruffled sleeves, a remnant from bygone days, circa 1940, Kim would guess. She had picked it up for $12.99 at some fleabag of an antique clothing store on Main Street in Santa Monica.

Kim loved it. "That has to be the world's most divine dress! It's perfect. Wear it."

"Everybody's going to be wearing designer originals, and she wants me to wear a dress I paid $12.99 for in some bargain shop," Jan said to the dress.

"Who's going to know what you paid for it, unless you wear a price tag? It *looks* like a designer original. I mean it. It *does*," Kim protested.

Jan went into the closet to see if she could find a pair of shoes that would go with the dress. Kim started checking out the pile of stuff on the bed. Jan sure had nifty taste, and not just in home decor. Since she'd become part of this family, Kim's wardrobe had improved markedly.

"Anybody home?" her father called up the stairs. He came bounding into the room. Exuberant, like a young boy, not a middle-aged man of forty-one. But that was her father, perennially young. One thing she knew for a fact: *he'd* never turn into one of those boring old fuddy duddies like some fathers. Everything about him was young: his looks, his attitude, his interests. Kim thought she'd have hated one of those old-fashioned-type fathers.

"Where's Jan?" he asked, coming to give Kim a kiss hello. Kim pointed to the closet. He tiptoed in and Kim heard Jan's startled exclamation. The two of them were smooching in there. They'd been married two years and still were like newlyweds. Kim thought that was pretty terrific; also a far cry from the way things had been around here a few years ago. It was a good marriage. A *great* marriage. Just like the one she and Brad would have someday. Brad was the only subject her father was a little less open-minded about, but Kim knew that was only because he was her father and slightly overprotective. He thought she was much too young to be seriously involved with someone.

One thing that helped was that Brad was at UCLA, her father's alma mater. Until recently she had taken it for granted it would be hers, too, but her father had talked her into applying to Stanford University, the best school in the state. *It's a school full of geniuses*, she reminded herself apprehensively. She was no genius, just a hard worker. But on paper she looked like a genius, a real overachiever. She wouldn't be surprised if Stanford accepted her, and that would be a problem. She didn't really want to go, but she couldn't very well turn down the best school in the state, could she? Anyway, her father wouldn't hear of it. As far as he was concerned, she was already in.

"How did the audition go, baby?" her father asked, emerging from the closet.

"Okay," she replied, escaping out the door.

"Should I open a bottle of champagne?" he called after her.

"Sam, drop it. She's a little upset," Kim heard Jan whisper.

"Wait a minute. Upset? Upset about what?" He came out into the hallway after her. "Hey, what's going on?"

"Nothing, Daddy. Sanders just isn't telling us who got the parts until Monday."

"That's not his style, is it?" he asked.

She shook her head. "No. Listen, no biggy. So, I'll find out Monday, that's all. Daddy, I almost forgot. If it turns out Richard Gere's at that thingee tonight, don't forget you promised to try and get his autograph for me," she added. "Just tell him to sign, *'To Kim, with fond memories. It was great while it lasted. Love, Dick.'*"

Seven

Why was she so uptight? That was easy. She knew her father would be upset if she didn't get the part. But she was going to get it, so what was the problem? *You're doing it again,* she told herself sternly, *worrying unnecessarily, making up things to worry about that don't exist.* But Sam was so proud of her, always bragging to everybody about his daughter, the future superstar — his brilliant, talented, beautiful daughter. To say he had a rather unrealistic image of her would be an understatement, but she tried to live up to it. She would die rather than disappoint him. He took such an interest in her and everything about her. Jodi said he was neurotically over-involved with her and her life, but Jodi didn't understand. Until Jan had come along, all they had was each other, just the two of them. They had depended on one another, spent all their time together after her mother left, turning to one another for solace and support. It was perfectly natural for them to be a little closer than most fathers and daughters.

"What do you think?" Jan asked, coming into Kim's room to model the dress. It looked sensational on her. With her silver kid evening slippers, she looked elegant and fashionable. Jan wasn't classically pretty, but she was strikingly attractive with her tawny blond hair, green eyes, and terrific figure. She had style, her own, unique, individual style. She knew it and played it up. She wasn't afraid to take chances and wear things that were different and unique. It was evident from the way she dressed, carried herself, and acted, that she felt good about herself.

Sam looked smashing in his tuxedo. Most men looked silly in them, like headwaiters or theater ushers, but he looked debonair, very suave, and right at home in his.

Sam and Jan had lots of things in common, including the fact that they were both nutty about clothes. But they had very expensive taste. They couldn't afford the kinds of things they liked, so, rather than do without them, they bargain shopped. Their idea of a scintillating Saturday was spending ten straight hours combing the discount stores downtown, sniffing out incredible bargains, designer originals for a fraction of their retail cost. Kim wouldn't be caught dead spending her time that way, but she didn't mind it a bit when Jan came home with something for her that she had picked up for next to nothing at Boynton's or Discount Dan's, or one of those other dives downtown.

"You guys look like movie stars!" Kim declared.

"You *are* going to eat something, aren't you?" Jan asked.

"Yes, I'm going to eat something."

"I've heard that one before," Jan said knowingly.

"I'll take an oath, okay? I hereby swear I will eat something. There! Satisfied? Go already, will you? Daddy's chomping at the bit. He can't wait to get there so he can show you off." Kim waved them off, then panicked. *Homework!* she thought, forcing herself to go back to her science project. She had two articles to write for the newspaper, and she hadn't even started them. When was she going to fit that in? Her stomach was growling. It would be better to take a break and, while she was at it, phone Jodi. No, better not take the time. She'd call Jodi later. She could save more time by taking her dinner back upstairs with her and eating it while she worked. She was engrossed in a chapter on the Plantagenets of England — evil King Richard III, his sidekicks, and the doomed twin boy princes imprisoned in the Tower of London — when the phone rang. It was Brad calling to say he was going to Fat City to pick up some ice cream for the troops and ask if she wanted him to drop some off for her. Ice cream was her favorite thing in the world, next to him. He knew she'd never be able to resist.

"All right, but you can't stay. You have to leave immediately."

"Of course! I'll just drop it off, then split," he promised, then added, "ten minutes."

"Ten minutes, my eye!" she said to the telephone. Brad had a problem. He was never on time. By this time, after going with him for two years, she knew he couldn't be. Not if his life depended on it. Her father said it was a sign of immaturity, and that if Brad had any consideration for others, he would learn to be on time. It wasn't the only thing about Brad her father disapproved of. Brad knew he wasn't Sam's favorite person in the world, and that made him very uncomfortable.

Well, Kim thought, *Brad is predictable.* She always knew, if he said he was going to arrive at a certain time, she could tack about an hour and a half onto that time and know exactly when he would show up.

She could thank Mr. Sanders for playing Cupid and bringing her and Brad together. In that fateful production of Gilbert and Sullivan's *Pirates of Penzance*, Brad, who had been a big deal around school, and in the drama club, had been cast as the pirate king. During the first readthrough, when the cast and crew had been assembled onstage going over the script for the first time, Kim had sat next to him. She had gone through the weeks of rehearsals in a state of suspended animation living for those moments when he would notice her; look in her direction, even accidentally; or speak to her — usually to say something like, "What's my next line?" or "Do you have an extra copy of the script?" He was so charming that all the girls were in love with him and he was in love with all of them in return. Never in a million years would it have occurred to Kim that Brad could ever be attracted to a plain, nondescript nobody like her. Then, on opening night, when the cast was taking one last curtain call, he grabbed her hand, squeezed it almost to the point of breaking it, and whispered fiercely, "Kim, I can't pretend any longer. I'm wild about you!" They had been together ever since.

Everyone kept reminding her that the chances of high school sweethearts staying together permanently were practically nil, but she and Brad intended to blow all the statistics and do it.

She checked her watch. Typical. It had been an hour already, and there was no sign of him. He'd have an excuse: a flat tire, engine trouble, a stray dog in the street he had to rescue — there was always a logical reason. An hour and twenty minutes from the time he called her he finally showed up, ridden with guilt, abjectly apologetic.

"I had to drop Brett off at his girlfriend's house, and he neglected to tell me that she lives all the way out in the boonies. Chatsworth," he said, following her into the kitchen.

"A likely excuse!" Kim said, pretending anger.

"It's true."

"It always *is*." She took the bag of ice cream from him.

Furtively he glanced around. "Anybody home?"

"As if you didn't know, you sneak!"

"Who, *me*? I'm hurt to the quick!"

She opened the bag. Peanut Butterscotch and Marshmallow Fudge Banana? She got two tablespoons from the silverware drawer, handed one to him, and used the other to attack the open carton of Peanut Butterscotch. *Not bad. Not bad at all.* "First one to finish the carton gets the prize," she said, digging in.

He scooped out a spoonful. "Which is?"

"The other carton, dummy! Eat. Then you have to leave. I have to get back to work."

"You think you might consider parting with one measly kiss? I am starved for affection, not ice cream," he pointed out.

She held him at arm's length. "Oh no you don't! You think because you brought me ice cream I'll let you stick around."

"Well, you must admit this is a lot more fun than trigonometry," he said and kissed her.

"*Out!*" she protested vehemently, trying to maneuver him toward the door. "I've got to finish my homework."

He sighed and shook his head. "What would happen if you didn't get the top marks in the class once?"

"I'd blow my brains out."

"Very funny! You know, you sound as though you mean that. You really want me to leave?"

"That's the general idea."

"Rejection, rejection! You don't know what this is doing to my ego."

"Oh, it's in top shape. It'd take a lot more than that to affect *your* ego. Maybe you ought to get yourself a girlfriend for weeknights. Me on weekends, her on weeknights. You'd have every night of the week covered," she suggested, smiling at him.

"I think I'll pass," he replied and kissed her one last time. "I'd rather just have *you* and have to share you with Dickens, Pythagoras, and the Norman Conquest, than have any six other girls I wouldn't have to share at all."

"You sure of that?"

"Positive!"

"It's nice to be appreciated."

"Oh, you *are*. And I'd appreciate you even more if I had more of you to appreciate. We really aren't spending much time together lately, Kim. I miss you," he said in a more serious tone, drawing her into his arms. She snuggled against him. It felt good to be held. She wanted him to stay. But she had to be strong and resist. Too much was at stake.

"Ten more minutes. Then I promise I'll

leave," he murmured and wrapped her more tightly in his arms. *Resist!* her built-in warning system screamed at her, and a little red light inside her head flashed on and off. "You are leaving now!" she announced, propelling him toward the living room. "And *I* am going back upstairs to work."

E^{ight}

Jan and Sam came home after midnight and stopped by Kim's room to say good-night. Jan tossed a menu on her desk. It had some writing on it. *To Kim — Best regards, Richard Gere.*

"Oh, my gosh, you got it!" Kim exclaimed, grabbing the menu and kissing it.

"Oh, my heartthrob!" her father said in a falsetto voice, imitating her.

"Daddy, nobody says that anymore. Heartthrob? That was fifty years ago. What does he look like?" she asked Jan, clutching the menu to her bosom. "Is he gorgeous?"

"Not really. His nose is kind of, um, *large*, shall we say? And he's not very tall," Jan replied and bent down to remove one shoe. "Oooh, my poor feet! My boss ought to pay me time-and-a-half for overtime — service above and beyond the call of duty. I danced my rear end off, and in these shoes it was sheer agony."

"I thought you were going to get to bed early?" Kim's father said to her.

She shrugged and muttered, "I thought I was, too."

Jan took off her other shoe. "By the way, I forgot to tell you. There's going to be a part-time summer job in my department if you're interested," she said to Kim.

"If I'm interested? Who wouldn't be interested? A job at a movie studio? You're putting me on!" Kim squealed, jumping up and running over to hug her.

"I get the impression she's interested," Jan said to Kim's father.

"I thought we were going to hold off on telling her," he replied.

"*You* were. I wasn't," Jan replied, looking at Kim.

"I'd really rather you didn't work this summer, baby," he said.

"But, Daddy, a job at a movie studio? What everybody in the world wants but hardly anybody ever gets? Listen, not that I'll get it. There'll be tons of people applying. What chance do *I* have? I don't even have any experience or anything."

"If you want it, you'll get it," Jan said, then scowled angrily at her feet. "Traitors! What'd I ever do to *you* except pamper you and indulge you, and now look how you repay me."

"You do enough during the school year,

baby. You ought to take the summer off," Kim's father said, pursuing the subject.

"But, Daddy, what will I do all summer, sit here all alone twiddling my thumbs? Brad and Jodi are both working. I don't even have wheels to go someplace, like to the beach. Or *anywhere*."

"We can work that out," Jan put in. "Your father can always drive me to work, and you can use my car."

"I hate doing that, Jan. You need it. Besides, I really *want* to work. I never had a job, and I've been dying for one. Everybody else works. Practically every kid in my class has some sort of part-time job. It'd be so neat earning my own money, and I could help out with some of the expenses. Don't tell me you guys wouldn't like *that*. Things have been pretty tight around here lately, and if I make Stanford, they're going to get a lot tighter."

Her father looked offended. "That's not your problem. I can handle my finances very nicely without your having to hold down a job."

"Daddy, I didn't say you couldn't, just that *I'd* like being able to earn a little for once, that's all. I know I don't *have* to, but I'd *like* to. It'd be fun."

"You won't think so a few years down the line when you have no choice," he muttered under his breath. "Be young and enjoy yourself while you still can, baby. Time enough to take on grownup responsibilities when you're a grownup."

She wanted to say, "But I *am* one, Daddy," only she didn't. "It's sort of silly to argue, being that the chances of my getting the job are about a zillion to one," she said.

Jan waved a shoe at her. "Oh, the odds are a lot better than *that*. You want it? You'll get it."

"What makes you say that? How could you possibly know?" Kim asked.

"Easy!" Jan said and smiled blandly at her. "I'm doing the hiring."

Kim burst out laughing. "Nothing like having friends in the right places," she said to her father. He didn't look too pleased, but he didn't pursue the subject further. That was a good sign. He could have just said no and squelched the whole thing right then and there. This way it was left open-ended.

"You really ought to get to bed," he said on his way out of the room.

Jan limped after him, turning back in the doorway to smile at Kim and say, "Maybe you'll be sorry after you find out what a slave driver I am."

"Some slave driver! Just like you are around here, huh? Listen, I hope you *do* make me work hard. That way I'll really learn. That's what I want. What's the sense of doing a job if you don't wind up learning something?"

"Oh, you'll learn all right. You'll also work

your adorable rear end off, but I forgot. You *thrive* on that. My boss will be ecstatic, to say nothing of shocked. He has this idea that all teenagers are lazy, shiftless, spoiled rotten, and unprincipled like *his* kids. Just wait till he meets you! He may never get over it. His kids may not either," she added, chuckling to herself, on her way out the door.

How really clever of you to get the world's greatest lady for a stepmother, you sly dog you, Kim thought, grinning to herself. Her first job, and not just *any* job. A job at a movie studio. Wait until Jodi heard. She'd turn green with envy. Kim would work real hard, impress Jan's boss. Then he might wind up hiring her after the summer on a part-time basis. If she wound up at UCLA, she could keep on working part-time, work her schedule around her job. The job would help out with some of the expenses. She'd feel good knowing she was making some sort of a contribution. Brad would go bonkers when she told him. He was always saying he wished he could work at a studio.

"What was your first job in Hollywood?" Johnny Carson would ask her when she appeared on his show. Naturally he would be talking about her first *acting* job, but, strictly speaking, her first acting job wouldn't have been her first job in Hollywood.

She would say, *"Oh, it was a part-time summer job in the publicity department at United Artists. I'll never forget how excited I was walking into the office the first day, meeting all those famous people, big movie stars. I was a kid with big ideas and no experience, but I learned fast."*

"Wasn't that where you were discovered?" Johnny would ask next, and she would tell him about how some big shot producer walked into the office one day, saw her sitting at her desk eating a tuna fish sandwich, flipped out completely over her, and carted her off that very instant for a screen test.

"Only he wasn't really the one who first recognized my talent," she would say, giving credit where it was due, remembering the other people who had helped her get where she was. *"If not for a teacher I had in high school named Sheldon Sanders, I wouldn't have known I had talent to begin with. He was the one who first told me I had the makings of a great actress."*

Maybe Johnny would surprise her by bringing Sanders on the show, like a reunion or something. Sanders, her father, Jan, Brad. . . . What about her mother? Would she be there, too? *"These are my mothers. It just so happens I have two of them,"* Kim would inform Johnny, *"but I only have one father, and he's the best, most wonderful father anyone ever had! He used to be an actor, too, but he had to give it up. If he'd been able to hang in there he probably would have been another Sir Laurence Olivier!"*

Nine

"Aren't you going to have breakfast?" Jan called to her when she dashed past the kitchen next morning.

Kim kept on going. "I'll get some at school," she called back on her way out the door. She wouldn't, but Jan didn't have to know that. She was down on her about her erratic eating habits as it *was*. For a stepmother, not a real one, she was awfully maternal. Too bad she and Kim's dad had decided they didn't want any more kids. She would have been great with little kids. Kim's father thought he was too old to start a new family. Big deal! Forty-one wasn't old. Lots of people started families in their late thirties and forties. But he was convinced it wouldn't be fair to the kids having a father so much older than everybody else's. "You could lie about your age. Nobody would ever know," Kim had told him when he had said that. "You look closer to thirty-one than forty-one, and Jan's just the right age at twenty-six."

Come to think of it, Jan might even be a little on the young side. Kim didn't think she would be ready for motherhood at twenty-six. Stardom, yes, but motherhood? Anyway, age didn't matter as much as aptitude. Kim wasn't positive about Jan — she was probably cut out to be a mother — but she knew for a fact that her father was a super father. Who was in a better position to judge that than Kim?

She slid in behind the wheel of Jan's Pontiac Firebird, a nifty car, especially in fire-engine red. Jan adored this car, which made it even more generous for her to let Kim borrow it. Pulling out of the driveway Kim felt a stab of pain, like a dull thud, behind her eyes and thought, *Oh, no! Not another headache.* How many did that make this week? She had lost count. Lately she just seemed to have a headache all the time, one long, uninterrupted headache. It was no wonder, since she was getting so little sleep. Last night was the perfect example, a typical night in the life of Kimberly Stanton, over-extended overachiever. She had planned on getting to bed early, but had she gotten to bed early? No! Did she *ever* get to bed early? Almost never. So, what was she going to do about rectifying the situation? Very little, if things kept up the way they were going lately. Even less than *that* once rehearsals started for *Kiss Me, Kate!*

That thought made her nervous, especially in the light of what she was about to do. Was she making a mistake? Probably, but since when had that ever stopped her from doing something she had made up her mind to do? Maybe she ought to discuss this with Jodi. If Jodi said it wasn't a good idea, Kim would scrap it. If she *did*, it would be a ghastly weekend.

Sanders must really be afraid of losing his job if he would do a thing like this to them, knowing how it felt. Either that, or this was his way of proving to them how right he was when he said acting was the toughest profession in the world. That could be it. He was always telling them that the only way they would ever really learn anything was from experience. Maybe he had decided to illustrate that fact by making them experience, on a lesser level, how it felt to be up for a part.

If that was it, he was redeemed in her eyes, but if it was that he was afraid of losing his job, and he was trying to protect himself, she was hugely disappointed in him.

She avoided the freeway and took the back roads to Jodi's. She liked to drive. Alone behind the wheel was the one time she was stationary, not frantically dashing around trying to do twenty things at once or riveted at a desk, concentrating with a fervor on some task or other. It was the one time when she could just sit still and do nothing but guide an efficient, high-powered machine to where she wanted to go and do some thinking. She pulled into Jodi's driveway. Since she was early, she indulged in one of her favorite daydreams, the one in which she won her first Oscar. She'd be sitting out there in the audience on Academy Award night, her father on one side of her, Brad on the other. She'd be hyperventilating, but she would appear to be calm, cool, and collected. The emcee would be announcing the names of the nominees for best performance by an actress in a leading role. Her name would be among them, of course. She would hold her breath, waiting. The TV camera would capture the moment for posterity as, with trembling hands, the emcee would tear open the envelope and, while a hush fell over the assemblage, read the winner's name: *"And, for the best performance by an actress in a leading role, MS. KIMBERLY STANTON!"*

Thinking about it gave her goosebumps. There would never be another moment in her life quite like that one, because no matter how many Oscars she won during the course of her long, distinguished career, nothing could ever equal the thrill of receiving that first one. In a voice fraught with emotion, she would thank just one person and one only, the one whose loving support and friendship, and unfailing belief in her, had sustained her through all the struggling and the disappointments along the way — her beloved co-star and husband, famous in his own right, Bradley E. Berson.

"What about *me*?" Jodi wailed when Kim told her about her acceptance speech. "Aren't you going to thank me, too?"

"Ahem! Ladies and gentlemen of the Academy, and guests, I want to thank my best friend, Jodi Alicia Adams, a pain in the rump who, for the past twenty-odd years, has never stopped nagging and badgering me, and driving me crazy, for two minutes," Kim laughed.

Jodi's stomach growled noisily. "I'm dying of hunger. Let's stop and have some breakfast."

"Can't. Something I have to do before homeroom," Kim murmured.

"Like what? What's more important than eating?"

"To *you*? Nothing, obviously, but to me, um, well . . . what d'you think about my going to see Mr. Sanders right now, asking him straight out if I got the part or not? Or should I just let it be and wait 'til Monday?"

Jodi deliberated, chewing on her lip. "Um, well, it would take the pressure off. Then maybe you could enjoy the weekend. Also I don't think it's fair that you have to suffer because of his mistake. He should have told you yesterday. All in all I'd say you're right to do it, yeah."

"You don't think he'll think I'm acting like a spoiled brat asking for preferential treatment?" Kim asked.

"Yes, but what's *that* got to do with anything? You *should* get preferential treatment.

You paid your dues, didn't you?" Jodi declared vehemently.

When they got to school, Jodi made a beeline for the cafeteria, grumbling about how she'd probably wind up with ptomaine poisoning at the very least, and Kim headed for the English department. Mr. Sanders was already there, in his office going over some papers. He looked up and smiled at her when she walked in.

"Funny. I was just thinking about you," he said. One of the secretaries stuck her head in the door to ask if he wanted coffee. He nodded at her and gestured Kim toward a chair. Kim sat down and cleared her throat nervously. "As a matter of fact, I was about to write a note to send to your homeroom teacher asking him to send you in for a chat," he went on.

"I must have gotten your brain waves. It's ESP," she said.

He smiled. "I wouldn't be at all surprised. I've always thought I was psychic. Look, Kim, I feel terrible. It was wrong of me not to tell the group who was going to play the lead parts. Thoughtless of me. I just wasn't thinking. I should have known better. You especially have enough pressure and stress to deal with as it *is*. You don't need me to give you more. Really, I've never seen anyone do as much as you do, Kim, get involved in so many things, and do them all to perfection. But, you must admit, you *are* pretty overextended at this point."

He looked at Kim, his eyes pleading with her to understand. "Hey, I chose *Kiss Me, Kate!* with you in mind for the part of Kate, but I've been checking your records. I don't know how you could possibly do it. Really, I don't. It looks to me as though you've got way too much to do as it is. I feel, if I give you the part, it will be more than you can deal with; it may even wind up making you ill, what with all those other things you have to do. I wouldn't want to be responsible for your getting sick, Kim, and this *is* my responsibility, my decision. . . ."

"Mr. Sanders, if you'll just listen to me for a minute," she interrupted, but he refused to listen and went on talking, telling her how hard it had been for him to come to a decision, how much he cared about her and her welfare, what a difficult position this put him in. She knew what was coming. Apprehension mounted inside her.

Finally he got around to it and said, "Kim, I'm going to give the part of Kate to someone else; someone who really needs it, who needs the experience, the exposure, the confidence. . . ." He kept on talking, explaining his decision, trying to rationalize it. Kim thought, *Who is he trying to convince, me or himself?* She knew the real reason he was doing this, and it had nothing to do with her being overextended. She got up and ran out of the room, down the corridor and into the women's lavatory, where she locked herself in one of the stalls. Around here that was one of the few places you could get any privacy, and even there it was hard.

Someone came into the lavatory bringing a cloud of cigarette smoke with them. Smoking was against the rules, but no one let that bother them. The smoke was choking her. She would be late for homeroom if she didn't get going. She unlocked the door and stepped out of the stall.

"Hi! Knew it was you. Recognized your tennis shoes," Margie Kaplow said, blowing smoke in her face. Kim went over to the sink and splashed some cold water on her face. She looked awful. Why was Margie looking at her that way? Hadn't she ever seen anyone cry before? People did it all the time. It was a basic human biological function when under stress, but maybe Margie thought Miss Perfect wasn't capable of tears, that she only cried when she was playing a part up on a stage in front of an audience.

A couple of girls came in. Kim escaped out the door. Her head was pounding. Should she go to the nurse's office? Better still, why not sign herself out and go home? Honor students were entitled to do that on occasion if they needed to, and she needed to.

She scribbled a note and stuck it in Jodi's locker. In Mr. Biggar's office, on the sign-out sheet in the explanation column, she wrote, "*bad headache*." Migraine described it more accurately. She knew all about those. Her mother had had enough of them. She was immobilized for days, totally closed off from the world. Kim's father had said they were psychosomatic and that her mother was inventing them in order to get attention. Could a person invent that kind of pain? Could she have inherited the tendency?

She pulled into the driveway, dragged herself out of the car, and stumbled into the kitchen, stopping to take two aspirin before going upstairs. She pulled down the shades. She wanted the room dark. The light hurt her eyes. She lay in bed waiting for the aspirin to work, praying that it would work. If she could just sleep, she told herself, listening to the pounding inside her head, maybe she would get through the day.

Ten

The sound of footsteps on the stairs woke her. Jan stuck her head in the door and said worriedly, "What's wrong? Are you sick? What are you doing in bed?"

"I had a headache, so I left school early, before homeroom. What time is it? I think I slept all day," Kim mumbled groggily and sat up.

"It must have been an awfully bad headache for you to leave school," Jan said, coming over to feel her forehead for fever. "Are you coming down with something? You're pale. Don't get up. What do you want? Whatever it is, I'll get it for you."

"I was thinking I ought to eat something. I haven't. Not since last night," Kim said and yawned.

"Oh, Kim, really! Why do you do that? You know how bad it is for you to skip meals.

Look, I'll bring something up for you. Name it." Kim nodded weakly.

Jan left, and Kim swung her legs over the side of the bed and sat there for a moment. The headache had subsided substantially. Now it was just a dull ache behind her eyes, the same one she had wakened with this morning — *every* morning lately, she reminded herself.

She made her way downstairs to the kitchen feeling weak and shaky, as though she had just gone through a long and serious illness. The mail lay on the countertop. There was a letter from her mother. Jan was watching her. Kim knew what she was thinking, that she was turning into an *anorectic* or something. *Anorexia nervosa.* Kim knew a girl who had it. She was seeing a therapist.

"I just forget to eat sometimes. I get involved in something, and I forget," she said, watching Jan drop two pieces of whole wheat bread into the toaster. "It's an advanced case of absentmindedness, not anorexia nervosa." She sat down at the table and put her chin on her hands. Jan went to get the butter and jam out of the refrigerator. "I went to see Mr. Sanders this morning to ask him to tell me if I got the part or not. Guess what? I didn't. According to him, I'm vastly over-extended, and it could be the straw that breaks the camel's back. Guess I'm the camel."

The toast popped up. Jan stood there staring fixedly at it for a full minute before she took it out of the toaster and dropped it on a plate. She put the plate down in front of Kim, who very carefully spread butter, then homemade blackberry preserves on a piece.

"I *am* doing a lot, but I could have handled it," Kim said and took a bite of toast. *How* was another question, but she didn't answer it. Didn't even want to think it, but it kind of snuck in uninvited.

"After leading you to believe the part was yours, I think it's awful of him to do this!" Jan declared, slamming the honey down on the table so hard the tea spilled. "Couldn't you talk to him, tell him how much this part means to you? Maybe he'll change his mind."

"Shelly Sanders? No way! Besides, I'm not about to beg him. I have *some* pride," Kim protested, pouring herself some tea.

"It just isn't fair!" Jan exclaimed.

"Haven't you noticed? An awful lot of things aren't, but we've still got to live with them," Kim sighed. Jan looked at her. They were both thinking the same thing, but neither of them wanted to say it. "Look, actors go through this all the time. It comes with the territory," Kim went on. "If you can't take disappointment and rejection, you shouldn't be an actress. Daddy's going to be awfully upset," she added as an afterthought. "He was counting on my playing this part. He was even talking about inviting some of the bigwigs from the studio to come to opening night."

"Yes, I know. He told me. His daughter, the star," Jan said a little irritably. Kim glanced up at her, taken aback. "Well, it puts you in the position of having to live up to all those things he says about you," Jan went on. "Not that you can't, but, well, I don't see why you should always feel you have to. Did you hear what you just said? *Daddy will be upset.* Never mind Daddy. What about *you*? He wasn't counting on playing Kate. *You* were. It's *your* disappointment, but it's not your failure," she added pointedly, staring Kim down.

"What's that supposed to mean?" Kim asked, feigning innocence, and pouring more tea.

"Just that you have a tendency to feel, when you don't come out Number One, the winner, the best, that you've failed him. Not an awfully realistic attitude, Kim. You know that, don't you? You can't always be Number One, the best at everything. Life doesn't work that way. Sometimes you come in second, or tenth, or hundredth. So long as you do your best, the best you're capable of doing, that's all that matters. Your father has high standards and expectations — for himself, for you, for everybody. If he puts that sort of pressure on himself, it's up to *him*, but it's not fair his imposing it on *you*."

"Imposing it on *me*? Jan, I don't know what you mean," Kim protested.

"Yes, you *do*. Kim, you have a tendency to close yourself off from people, people who love you and care about you," Jan said very quietly. Kim dropped her eyes. She focused on a spot on the tile floor where a ladybug was laboriously making its way toward the table leg. What Jan said was true, and she knew it. She *did* have a tendency to close herself off, especially when she was troubled. Why did she do that? She had no idea. But she *did* know that a lot of the time she wasn't being herself at all. She was putting on an act, pretending to be someone else, hiding her true feelings under a mask.

"I don't know why I do it," she said in a choked voice.

"Maybe because you aren't sure you can really trust people, and you don't like being vulnerable, letting them know too much about you. Maybe it's because you don't think the real you is all that lovable," Jan ventured. Kim stared at the floor. Maybe it was something else, too, because she was afraid people would find out she wasn't the person she advertised herself as being, the person everybody looked up to and envied and wished they could be like — Miss Perfect.

The ladybug had reached the table leg and was making its way up it, slowly but surely. It had a goal, and it knew what it wanted — to get to the top of the table, obviously. It was extremely singleminded in its quest.

"Open up, Kim," Jan said, standing beside her. "Take a chance and let people know you, the *real* you, not the one who's playing a part. You might get hurt sometimes, but you might also find out that people are a lot nicer, more loving and trustworthy than you think."

Eleven

Kim was about to reply when the door flew open, and Jodi bounded in, looking like Raggedy Ann in her white overalls and red-and-white checkered shirt with her hair in pigtails. "That was some note you left me. *'Running away from home. Will write if I get work!'* What's *that* supposed to mean, if you don't mind my asking?"

"Nothing, really. I was in an enigmatic mood," Kim replied.

"I thought maybe you and Brad were eloping or something," Jodi declared, flopping down in a chair.

"I had a headache, so I decided to come home," Kim told her.

"Would you like something, Jodi?" Jan asked and listed the possibilities, starting with the top shelf of the refrigerator and going on from there.

"Don't mind if I do," Jodi said.

"We'll finish our discussion later, okay?" Jan said to Kim, who nodded mutely, thinking that a person couldn't get away with much with Jan. She was relentless.

"If you boiled these overalls, you'd get great soup," Jodi said disgustedly, checking herself out. "How did I get so dirty?"

"If I know you, you were probably playing touch football with the guys after school," Kim replied.

Jan held up a jar of peanut butter from the refrigerator. Jodi went into ecstasy. Next to pizza, it was her favorite food. "Don't bother putting it on anything. I don't need a plate. Just give me a spoon, and I'll eat it out of the jar," she said to Jan. "I'm very particular about what kind of peanut butter I eat. It has to be made from peanuts. This looks just right." Jan handed her the jar and a spoon, and Jodi dug in. "So, what happened when you went to see Sanders?" she said, her voice muffled by the peanut butter.

"Oh, that. Well, I asked him to tell me if he was giving me the part or not, and he told me. Oh, yeah, he told me all right. *Did* he! It turns out — are you ready for this? — he's not."

Jodi almost choked on a spoonful of peanut butter.

"Yeah, I know, I was a little surprised myself," Kim informed her and got up and went to the refrigerator to get her some milk before she choked to death.

Jodi swallowed, took a minute to unglue

her tongue from the roof of her mouth, then said, "You're not going to like my saying this, but I'm gonna say it anyway. . . ."

"I'm listening," Kim said.

"Whatever reason he's doing this for, I think he's doing you a big favor not giving you the part," Jodi declared, waving her spoon in the air to emphasize the statement. "How were you planning to fit the damned part in, anyway? You don't have enough time to fit in what you're already doing without *that*, too, and, besides, think of all the nights you won't be up till the wee hours rehearsing, all the weekends you won't have to give up. Think of Brad. You remember him, don't you? You and he may even get to see each other once in a while now that you're not going to have to play Kate. To put it bluntly, kiddo, now, thanks to Shelly Sanders, you *may* just wind up surviving your junior year of high school!"

Kim looked at Jan questioningly. "What do you think? As if I didn't already know."

"If you know, why are you asking?" Jodi demanded.

"She wants to hear me say it. Okay, I will," Jan said, peering intensely into Kim's eyes. "I think Jodi's right. He did you a favor. You never in a million years would have thought of turning it down if he'd given you the part, so he had to do it *for* you. He may not have saved your life, like Jodi said, but he may have helped both your physical and mental state by doing this." She picked up her pocketbook from the counter and headed for the door. "I have to go to the supermarket. Anything you girls want?"

"Now that you mention it," Jodi said, "a new car, a stereo, a color TV, a new wardrobe, a custom-made surfboard." Jan left. "She's super! You know what? You're damned lucky. Why don't we trade? You take my mom. I'll take Jan," Jodi said when Jan was out of earshot.

"Sorry. No deal. You think I don't know when I've got it good?" Kim replied. Her words were light, but at the moment Kim wasn't feeling all that warmly toward her stepmother. Like Jodi, Jan had a tendency to be ultra-outspoken at times. Not that she wasn't right, because usually she *was*, but there were some things Kim didn't like hearing, even when she knew they were true. Jan had never been quite this outspoken before, but then she must feel very strongly. She would never think of interfering otherwise.

"Hark! Methinks I hear a voice," Jodi said, cupping her ear with her hand, inadvertently getting peanut butter all over it.

"What's to eat?" Brad asked, charging into the room. He was wearing cutoffs with paint stains all over them and a T-shirt with ACTORS DO IT BETTER! written on the front, and, as usual, he was barefoot. Jodi studied the T-shirt.

"I wonder if they really do."

"Better believe it!" he declared.

"Vanity, vanity, all is vanity!" Jodi stated.

Brad looked at Kim. "What's wrong?"

"Nothing! What makes you think something *is*?"

"I'm psychic. Come on. Give!"

"Oh, all right, if you insist." She looked at Jodi. "I found out today I'm not getting the part."

"You *what*? You're putting me on!"

"No, I'm not. Read my lips, okay? *Sanders is not giving me the part.* He told me this morning. In no uncertain terms. I'm out. Scratch one leading role. Oh, well, I really didn't want to play Kate, anyway." Before Brad could say anything, Kim said in a level tone, "Forget it, okay? It's no big deal. Believe me, I can handle it. I'll have to. Anyway, I might as well get used to it. It comes with the territory, right?"

Brad said sarcastically, "What are you, in training for sainthood? You some kind of martyr, or what? Why are you being so good-natured about it? Why don't you scream, have a tantrum, run amuck or something?"

"Look, I could cry and scream, indulge in a glorious bout of self-pity. What good would that do? I'm still not getting the part, so why bother? Crying gives me headaches, and I've got one already, and I don't want it to get any worse, so . . . could we please talk about something else? This is really getting boring," she concluded.

Jodi and Brad were looking at each other. Kim hated the way they treated her, like some kind of wacko, like she wasn't quite all there.

Not too stable. Frail, poor thing. The slightest upset sets her off, so let's be careful not to say the wrong thing. Bull! She turned to smile at them. "Hey, you guys, surprise, surprise! Little Kimmy's not about to lose control, get hysterical, or do anything else along those lines. She's a lot tougher than you think, and you know what? She's going to get a lot tougher still from here on in. You better believe it!" Brad and Jodi looked skeptical.

When they left, Kim took out her mother's letter and tore open the envelope. In the letter her mother wrote that she was contemplating flying out for opening night of *Kiss Me, Kate!*

Kim thought, *I had better write quick and tell her not to come. She probably won't be panting to spend all that money to fly out here to see somebody else play the lead.* Okay, Kim would write. What was she feeling guilty about? It wasn't *her* fault she wasn't playing the part. She hadn't made the decision. Someone else had.

I can't just say she shouldn't come, she thought. She would have to explain the situation, then leave the final decision up to her mother. That way it wouldn't be her responsibility if her mother decided not to come.

Twelve

"Have a nice day, baby?" her father asked when they were having dinner.

Yeah, terrific! But a funny thing happened on my way to homeroom, Kim thought, reaching for the salad.

"Jan, honey, did we mail out the check for the telephone company this month?" he went on and helped himself to a piece of bread.

"Yes, Sam, we did," Jan replied and looked at Kim.

"Pass the butter, will you, Kim?"

"Sure, Daddy." Kim passed him the butter dish.

"So, tell me about your day. Anything interesting happen?" he went on.

"Yeah, one thing. I went to see Mr. Sanders, to ask him if he was giving me the part or not? And guess what he said? I don't get to play Kate!"

He was preoccupied and didn't really hear

her. Spreading butter on his bread, he murmured abstractedly, "What did you say, baby?"

"Sanders decided not to give me the part, Daddy," she said. "He says he *was* going to, but now he can't, in all conscience, because I'm so vastly overextended as it is, and, rather than burden me further, he'll give it to someone else," she added, imitating Sheldon Sanders' pitch that morning. Her father's reaction took her by surprise. Somehow she hadn't expected him to react so violently. He slammed down his knife, pounded the table with his fist, and bellowed, "Who the hell does that man think he is, promising you, then breaking his promise? Is that the way a teacher is supposed to behave, a person in authority, someone who's supposedly knowledgeable, an expert on dealing with kids?"

"Don't shout, Sam," Jan said, a slight edge to her voice. "Sanders is only doing what he thinks is right. Kim's exhausted. He knows that. He just thinks it would be too much for her, that's all."

"How the hell does *he* know whether it's too much for her. Why didn't he ask her if she thought it would be too much before he made his decision? The kid's a worker. She thrives on hard work, the more the better. She could have handled it, couldn't you, baby?"

Kim looked at Jan. She was about to say, "Sure, Daddy!" but instead she said in a low voice, "I'm not so sure I could have."

He stared at her, about to say something else, but Jan interrupted him. "Sam, she's been getting headaches lately, a lot of them. She looks exhausted. She can't keep her weight up."

"I'm just tired," Kim hastened to assure them. "Don't make more of it than it is. When you're tired, you get headaches and lose weight. It's perfectly logical."

"Is it?" Jan said in an ominous tone, shaking her head at her. Kim speared a slice of tomato with her fork. It was dripping with salad dressing. She put the fork down on her plate.

"I don't get enough sleep. That's the whole problem."

"That's what I keep telling you," her father said. "I'd be getting headaches, too, if I were only getting five or six hours of sleep a night. Brad expects you to go out every night, on weekends, too. Easy for him. He doesn't get up 'til noon."

"Daddy, I haven't seen Brad all week. It's not that. It's, well, never mind." She nibbled a lettuce leaf. What other things caused headaches, aside from galloping exhaustion? Brain tumors? Blindness? She could be going blind. She could see it now. A blind actress, only the parts she'd be able to play might be rather limited. On the other hand, if she was a really good actress, she could fake it. No one would ever know. Poor Brad, saddled for life with a blind wife, but he'd never forsake her. Not Brad — good, fine, noble, loyal, understanding Brad.

The phone rang. "I'll get it!" she exclaimed and made a mad dash for the phone.

"Why don't I come over later?" Brad asked hopefully.

"I'm going to sleep early tonight if it kills me!" she declared.

"It's going to kill *me*, not you," he muttered.

"Brad, I've got to get some sleep, I mean it."

"Couldn't I just come over for a little while? A couple of hours? One hour? A half an hour?"

She was about to relent when her father said, "Tell him you're going to bed early, and he shouldn't come over."

"So, what's on the agenda for tomorrow then?" Brad asked.

"I'm studying ..."

"For the SATs," he finished for her.

"Riiight!" Kim replied in a teasing tone.

"So, look, I'll see you sometime, like in about ten years or so."

"Brad, don't make me feel guilty," she said.

"Okay, okay. Sorry. It's just that I miss you and ... hell! Brett's going to a basketball game at Northridge. Guess I'll go with him," Brad said.

"But you hate basketball games," she reminded him.

"I know, but I like to suffer. I love you, heartless wench!" he said and hung up.

Thirteen

"It's a beach day," Jodi announced when she phoned first thing next morning.

"It's also the day I'm going to lock myself in my room and study for the SATs," Kim replied resolutely.

"A day at the beach would do you good in your present condition. Even *you* need recreation sometimes. Workaholics and computer brains need to take a day off, too," Jodi informed her. "Come to the beach. I bet, if you do, when you get back you'll feel so much better you'll zip right through the SATs *without* studying.

Kim laughed. The idea of zipping through any exam without studying was ludicrous. Jodi knew that better than she did. She never zipped through an exam, mainly because she rarely studied. Kim wavered. A day at the beach would be wonderful. She hadn't had a day off for ages, not in weeks, and Jodi was right — it *was* a beach day. She *could* study all day tomorrow.

No, she couldn't possibly go. Besides, she didn't even have a decent bathing suit to wear. The ones from last summer were in shreds.

"Call Brad and tell him to come with us," Jodi said as an inducement.

"He has classes on Saturdays," Kim replied, leaning over to open her bureau drawer, the one in which she kept her bathing suits and shorts. She had forgotten about the nifty little red number Jan had picked up for her at the end of the summer.

"I'll pick you up in a half an hour!" Jodi said and, before Kim could say a word, hung up. Kim put on the bathing suit, just to see if it still fit, and looked at herself in the mirror. No wonder Jan was worried about her. She looked skinny and so pale. Like a ghost. Ugh! How could she go out tonight with Brad looking like that? The beach would be gorgeous today. Some color would help a lot, especially with the dress she was wearing. She slipped on a pair of old jeans and a sweatshirt, grabbed a beach towel from the linen closet, and was outside when Jodi pulled up.

"Think old Sid'll make it to the beach?" she asked Jodi.

"Indubitably! He never breaks down on the way to the beach. Only on the way to work," Jodi giggled. The beach was pretty crowded, especially for February. They found an uninhabited patch of sand a little ways away from the crowd, spread out their beach towels, and stretched out. Jodi worked on her tan; Kim on a burn, which was all she ever got. Lobster red, that was her color.

"I'm getting antsy. Think I'll take a walk," Jodi said after about three seconds. She walked about six paces, then stopped to talk to a group of boys. Kim closed her eyes. *What a luxury just to lie here and do nothing.* She was glad she had come. She needed a day off desperately. Jan would be proud of her. *Mmm, the sun feels so good! I'm so tired lately. I slept all day yesterday* . . . she thought happily as she drifted off to sleep.

"For someone who's supposed to be brilliant, you sure don't think sometimes. Why didn't you put something over yourself if you were going to fall asleep in the sun? You're slightly vermillion," she heard Jodi saying when she came out of her sleep. Jodi was standing over her. "I didn't know I was going to fall asleep," she replied, touching her arm to feel how hot it was. It was as red as an apple. Her back was sore, too. She must have turned over in her sleep.

"You're going to hurt like anything. We'll stop on the way home for something, some lotion to put on it. Come on. Let's get you out of the sun," Jodi said, dragging her off the beach.

Kim staggered after her. "I've got some lotion at home. Have to be careful. Allergies."

"I'm going out with him," Jodi announced.

Kim was a little slow on the uptake. "Who?"

"Paul Newman!" Jodi said sarcastically. "Glenn Yancy. Who else did I spend the afternoon with?"

"Glenn Yancy? Who's Glenn Yancy?"

"The surfing champion. Don't tell me you've never heard of him."

"Oh, *that* Glenn Yancy," Kim yawned, wondering why she hadn't. "Tony will be delighted to hear it."

"He won't. Hear it, I mean," Jodi said, looking at her narrowly.

"Don't look at *me*! Not from *me* he won't. My lips are sealed," Kim said, wincing as her backside and the car seat collided. "Oooh, the back of my thighs are killing me. Can we stop somewhere for a cold drink? I'm dying of thirst," she asked as Jodi pulled out of the lot. They stopped at Aardvark's Ark, a health-food restaurant in the canyon where all the surfers hung out. She followed Jodi inside. "You're really going out with Glenn Yancy?"

"I said so, didn't I?"

"Jodi, how can you be so unprincipled?"

"It's okay. You've got enough principles for the two of us. Abundant principles," Jodi replied.

"You're supposedly going steady. If you want to go out with other guys, why go steady in the first place? That's not being overly principled, making a commitment, then sticking to it, or just not making it at all."

"Baloney! Things happen sometimes, and then it's just not feasible," Jodi countered.

"By feasible you mean convenient," Kim exclaimed. "If the first time another boy comes along, you want to go out with him, you shouldn't be going steady to begin with."

"Did anyone ever tell you you're a pain in the rump?" Jodi said sweetly.

"Like I'm always saying, you can dish it out, Adams, but you can't take it. You like telling everybody else what to do, but you don't like it when somebody tells *you*!" Kim pointed out.

Jodi swooped down on a table next to the window where they would be highly visible. "Plenty of boys have asked me out while I was going with Tony. I didn't go out with any of *them*. I'd have to be bonkers to turn down Glenn Yancy, wouldn't I? That'd be very self-destructive on my part. I'll have a veggieburger and a banana protein shake," she said to the waitress, a girl they knew from school — a senior named Marcie Berger.

"I'll have a veggieburger and iced herbal tea, about six of them," Kim said. Marcie was looking at her as though she thought she was going to burst into flames any second. She knew she looked like a fright with her hair sticky with sweat and this sunburn. Oh, well, aside from Marcie, no one knew her. She would have felt a lot more comfortable sitting at one of the other tables instead of here in the window like a department store mannequin on display.

"Aren't you glad you listened to me and came to the beach?" Jodi was saying. "You look so much more, um, *relaxed*."

"Redder, too. I may be hospitalized by nightfall, but I'm glad, I'm glad!" Kim muttered.

"There's Neil," Jodi said, pointing to a tall, gangly kid who rode through the doorway on a skateboard. Neil didn't have his driver's license yet, so that was his basic means of transportation. Neil spotted her and glided over.

"You got some burn! Gosh, doesn't it hurt?" he asked, looking at her chest.

"Not much," she replied. "Only when I laugh."

He looked a little perplexed. Jodi giggled inanely and, when he had glided off, whispered, "He's the cutest thing. It runs in the family."

"He's a little young for you."

"I like younger men."

"Younger, older. Men, period."

"Can I help it if I'm attracted to members of the opposite sex?"

"No, but every last one of them?"

On the way home they stopped at Jodi's to pick up her clothes for the dance, her makeup, and her trusty hair dryer. She was getting dressed at Kim's. Her parents were throwing her younger sister, Dinah, a birthday party. There would be twenty-five shrieking, squealing ten-year-olds, all girls, which was not Jodi's idea of a fun evening.

"Get me out of here! Don't you let those monsters in my room, or I'll take my tape recorder back," she said to Dinah.

"Dinah's gorgeous. She looks like you," Kim said when they were in the car. Jodi made a terrible face.

"Gorgeous if you dig overgrown Barbie dolls!"

"Now that you mention it, you *do* look a little like Barbie," Kim laughed. Was she imagining it, or was everything shrinking? Her eyes felt like hot coals. She couldn't stand the feel of the upholstered car seat against her back, and the backs of her legs were on fire.

"Brad's going to be thrilled. Hope he's not in an amorous mood. He's not going to be able to lay a finger on you tonight." Jodi nosed Sidney into Kim's driveway and turned the ignition off, but Sidney was in a recalcitrant mood and kept on going for a full minute, shimmying and shaking. "Maybe we'd better call the boys and tell them we can't make it," Jodi suggested, helping Kim out of the car. The house looked as if it was a million miles away, and it kept swaying back and forth.

"Stop that!" Kim said to it.

"Stop what? I'm not doing anything," Jodi said.

"I wasn't talking to you. Do you think a person can die from sunburn? Well, at least I won't look like Casper the Ghost anymore," Kim said, staggering up the front path.

Fourteen

"Kim, for goodness' sake, what did you do to yourself?" Jan exclaimed when she saw her.

"It's not as bad as it looks," Kim lied.

"Let me get you something to put on it," Jan said, heading for the first aid kit.

"No. I don't want to go to the dance smelling like a pharmacy. I'll be okay. Really. It doesn't hurt all that much."

"Liar!" Jodi said when they were upstairs in Kim's room.

"She's such a worrier. I don't want her to freak," Kim replied and went to look at herself in the mirror. No wonder everybody was hysterical. She wasn't just red. She was practically purple. She felt funny, kind of light-headed and out of it. How would she get through the evening? She couldn't cancel out on Brad again. She'd have to muddle through somehow. The shower made her feel a little better. Kim stood under the cold water for a long time. Maybe that would keep her from swelling up. Shampooing her hair was a major challenge. It hurt to raise her arms. They felt as though they weighed about fifty pounds each. Jodi helped her dry it and get into her underwear. Underwear hurt, but dresses hurt worse, and shoes were agony. She skipped the pantyhose, they would have been unbearable. She never would have been able to manage the makeup without Jodi's help.

"You don't need much. Just a little eyeshadow, mascara, and some lipstick. There! You look terrific, sunburn and all. That dress is fabulous!" Jodi breathed, stepping back to get the overall effect.

"Have I got time to lie down for a while?" Kim asked weakly and looked longingly at her bed.

"Don't you dare! In that dress? Just stand there. Don't move a muscle. Here's your purse. They'll be here any minute, so hang in there," Jodi assured her.

"You think so, huh? Then you don't know Brad," Kim muttered, standing still. Then, miracle of miracles, Brad was on time — through no fault of his own. He couldn't take the credit, since Tony was the one who was driving, not him. Brad looked gorgeous in tan slacks with pleats; a light pink, Oxford cloth button-down shirt; and a light blue Shetland sweater tied around his neck. For once he had on shoes. He gave her a questioning look. "Did you get that sunburn studying?" he asked wryly.

Her father walked in on his way to the kitchen. Right on cue, Brad started showing signs of extreme discomfort.

"Hi, Mr. Stanton," he stuttered and backed into a coffee table, nearly knocking over Jan's favorite lamp. On his way out the door he tripped over his own feet and nearly fell flat on his face. Kim was mortified.

"I don't believe you. What *is* your problem?" she asked when they were in the car.

"Sue me. Your old man intimidates me. He makes me feel like I'm six years old and extremely stupid," Brad replied coldly.

"But all he did was say hello. That makes you feel six and stupid, when someone says hello to you?"

"If the someone's your old man? Yeah!"

"Oh, really! I'm looking forward to going through life having you freak out every time my father walks into a room. That'll be lovely."

They spent the rest of the ride in silence. The dance was held in the boys' gym at the high school. It smelled awful, like perspiration and unwashed socks. Someone should have opened a couple of windows and let some fresh air in. Kim thought that would have helped. Jodi dragged Tony onto the dance floor. Kim squinted. Everything looked so funny, kind of far away and out of focus. Was that yellow object with Billy Raines, Margie Kaplow?

"You okay?" Brad asked solicitously, his mood forgotten.

"Fine."

"Want to dance?" he said.

"Why not? That's what we came here for, isn't it?" She hoped it wouldn't be a slow dance. If he touched her, she'd hit the ceiling.

"What'd you think of the band?" Jodi asked when she glided by.

"Oh, terrific, only the drummer's out of sync, the lead guitarist started playing the day before yesterday, and the singer can't carry a tune to save himself," Kim muttered.

"Aren't we in a charming mood tonight?" Brad said.

She smiled at him. Smiling hurt, so she stopped and scowled instead. "I'm always charming. Didn't you know?"

"Don't you feel well? Is it the sunburn?"

"The sunburn? What sunburn? I don't have a sunburn."

He touched her forehead with his lips. "You're burning up."

"Burning with love," she exclaimed. She couldn't bend her knees. Her ankles were swelling up, and the shoes were so tight she could hardly take a step. Jodi danced by again.

"You're swelling up!"

"Like a blowfish," Kim giggled and puffed out her cheeks.

"I'm taking you home!" Brad declared and, taking her by the arm, started leading her off the floor. Tony handed him the car keys.

"I'll come back for you guys," Brad told him. He drove home at a careful speed.

"I've got a sunburn, I'm not giving birth," she said irritably. Her father and Jan were planning a quiet evening at home alone together. They'd be thrilled when she walked in. They'd probably be delighted when she went off to college. Then they could be alone at last.

"I knew it! You should have stayed home in the first place. Look at you! You're all swollen. It's sun poisoning. I'm calling the doctor right now," Jan declared, heading for the phone.

"She's overreacting," Kim said to her father.

He put a hand on her forehead. "You're burning up."

"That seems to be the consensus of opinion. I'm sorry I ruined the evening," she said to Brad.

"Do you want me to stick around for a while?" he asked, looking at everything in the room except her father.

She shook her head. "Better get back to the dance. You can't leave Jodi and Tony stranded."

"It's okay. They won't want to leave yet."

"Just go, Brad, okay?" she said a little harshly. She could just picture him and her father left alone together in the living room.

"The doctor's on her way," Jan said, coming back into the room.

"I'll call you," Brad stammered, backing away.

"Yes, do that." Kim allowed herself to be propelled from the living room, up the stairs, into her room, where Jan helped her get undressed and into bed. She couldn't tolerate her pajamas touching her body, only the sheet. She lay on her back staring at the rosebuds that marched in diagonal lines across her ceiling. The lines kept shifting and moving. Marching rosebuds. Clever! Brad was upset. Who could blame him? Another boy would have been blowing a gasket right now, but he was so understanding, so easygoing and accepting. Sometimes she caught herself wishing he wasn't, that he'd get angry, take a stand, assert himself for once instead of always letting her have her way. Her father came into the room. He looked worried.

"A sunburn's nothing to get uptight about, Daddy," she assured him. She didn't add that a headache might be.

"I'm not worried. What makes you think I'm worried, baby?" he said, coming to sit beside her. He smoothed the hair off her forehead and smiled at her. "When you do something, you do it, don't you?"

"I wonder who I take after?"

"Mmm. Are you trying to tell me something?"

"Two peas in a pod, remember?"

"You could do worse."

"You're telling *me*? Daddy, Brad is so uncomfortable around you. Couldn't you make more of an effort to put him at ease?"

He looked surprised. "If he's uncomfortable, that's *his* problem. I've always been more than nice to the boy."

She nodded. She wanted to say something else, but she thought better of it. What was the use? He couldn't see that he was doing anything to incur Brad's negative feelings. "I wonder who Sanders will pick to play Kate," she mused, watching the rosebuds converge on the ceiling above her, and started telling him about the other girls who had auditioned.

"Whoever he picks, she'll never be able to play the part the way *you* would," he said, interrupting her. "I know how disappointed you are, baby. And I'm sorry."

"You're disappointed, too. You really wanted me to play that part," she ventured, watching his eyes.

He smiled and patted her hand. "Don't be silly, sweetheart. How could I be disappointed in *you*? It's just a part in a high school play, not Broadway or Hollywood. So, you don't get to do this one. There'll be plenty of others. Hundreds of them before you're through, and they'll be the real thing, not small-time stuff. Sanders made a big mistake not casting you as Kate, but that's *his* loss, not yours. You've got much bigger fish to fry," Sam pronounced philosophically.

Fifteen

Dr. Freed showed up looking sleepy and disgruntled. She gave Kim a thorough examination, checked out her eyes, ears, nose, and throat; listened to her heart and lungs; and generally investigated everything but the actual problem, her sunburn.

"How often have you been getting these headaches?" she asked.

"What headaches?" Kim replied, wondering how she knew about them.

"The ones your stepmother tells me you've been getting rather frequently lately," Dr. Freed replied.

"Oh, *those* headaches! About every other minute."

"Lately she just seems to have one all the time," Jan said.

"Any other symptoms?" the doctor inquired.

"I'm always tired. Is that a symptom, Doc?"

"Depends. Are you getting enough sleep?"

"No."

Dr. Freed turned to Kim's father and said, "Just to be on the safe side, Sam, I'd like to do a few tests."

He nodded. "What kinds of tests?" Kim piped in. After all, this *was* her body. She was entitled to know what they were planning to do to it.

"Oh, routine," Dr. Freed replied evasively. "A few blood tests."

"You want to find out if I have tired blood," Kim said and started doing the TV commercial for iron tablets. Dr. Freed was not amused.

"My office first thing Monday morning. Nine o'clock, and don't eat anything after midnight tomorrow night. You'd be wise to get some rest over the weekend, young lady."

"Doc, if I were *wise*, would I be here right now, lying here on my bed of pain looking like a blowfish?"

That one got a semi-smile out of the doctor, who said, on her way out the door, "I'm going to prescribe some lotion. That's quite a burn you've got there."

"Thirty bucks for her to tell me I've got a sunburn?" Kim said to Jan.

Kim wondered why Dr. Freed wanted to do those tests. Was it on account of the headaches? Headaches weren't anything to be alarmed about, were they? They could be just a symptom of something else, something a lot more dire. She had known a girl once, Laurie Ingraham. They had been in the same third-grade class in elementary school. Laurie was one of those kids who was always complaining about something or other. She complained steadily about headaches. After a while nobody paid any attention to her. They all thought she was just a chronic complainer. They didn't think that anymore when, in fourth grade, Laurie Ingraham died of leukemia.

"GIFTED YOUNG ACTRESS DIES AT AGE SIXTEEN." She'd do a dynamite deathbed scene: underplayed, very poignant.

Those rosebuds sure were active. Now they were dancing a polka on her ceiling. Was she imagining it, or did she hear bells ringing? Dancing rosebuds, bells — she really *was* in bad shape. The phone was ringing, but it wasn't ringing in her room. How come? She sat up and checked the phone. It was on her desk where it was supposed to be, but it wasn't plugged in. Someone had unplugged her extension. The phone just kept on ringing and ringing. Why didn't someone answer it? It must be Brad calling to find out how she was, and he was probably frantic.

She would have gotten up and plugged her extension in, only she didn't have the strength. Even if she could make it up out of this bed, she'd never make it all the way across the room to the desk. Poor Brad! He

sure put up with a lot from her. Having her
for a girlfriend was a trial, to say the least.
She had acted like a real idiot tonight. She
hated herself. Well, Jan had advised her to
stop covering up and let the real Kim Stanton
out. If that was the real Kim Stanton, she
wasn't sure she wouldn't be better off keeping her under wraps.

"Stop that!" she told the rosebuds. The
phone had stopped ringing. Someone had
answered it, she supposed. She closed her
eyes. She was tired! She felt as though she
could sleep for a week, a month, a year.

"You all right?" a voice said, and Jan
crept into the room. Her voice sounded as
though it was coming through a wind tunnel.
Kim opened her eyes, then closed them again.
They felt so heavy. She couldn't keep awake.

"Sleep," she murmured as she sank into
semi-consciousness. Jan came to stand beside her. She put a hand on Kim's forehead.
It felt cool. She leaned down and kissed Kim
very lightly on the cheek, then whispered,
"Goodnight, love. Sleep tight," and tiptoed
from the room.

Sixteen

"Breakfast is served!" Kim's father said, putting a tray on her lap. Orange juice, oatmeal, whole wheat toast with butter and marmalade, and herbal tea. It was a lot to eat for only one person.

"Don't get me wrong," she said to the tray. "You're extremely appealing, honestly, but I don't happen to be Arnold Schwarzenegger. I can't consume fourteen thousand marching calories at once, especially first thing in the morning on an empty stomach." She smiled at her oatmeal. Last night seemed like a bad dream. Had that horrible girl been *her*?

"The pharmacy sent that lotion the doctor prescribed for you," her father said, putting a bottle on the night table.

"Oh, I don't need it, Daddy. The burn's all better. I feel fine. See what a good night's sleep can do?"

"You certainly *look* better, a hundred percent better," he said, relieved.

"You didn't have to bring me breakfast in bed. I could've come down."

"I like to pamper you, baby. It gives me pleasure," he assured her and took a nibble of her toast.

"Help yourself. Never in a million years could I eat all this," she said, holding the plate out to him.

He shook his head and said, "Calories!"

"Daddy, you're a bean. Why're you always so worried about your weight?"

"I want to *stay* a bean, that's why. Eat! Or Jan will come up here and spoon feed you."

She laughed. "I know. What a mother hen she turned out to be."

"Don't knock it. The lady's wild about you. If it came to a choice, you or me, I do believe she'd pick you every time."

"If that were true, we'd all be in a lot of trouble," she said, her mouth full of oatmeal. Jan made it just right, creamy. Not too sweet.

It's amazing what lack of sleep could do to a person. Kim had felt crazy the night before, close to the edge. She had read somewhere about some tests some scientists had done to find out the effects of lack of sleep on people. It had affected them adversely, not just physically, but mentally and emotionally, too. They had concluded that if you went without sleep long enough, you could go right over the side into mental illness.

"Good?" Sam asked, watching her enjoy her oatmeal.

She nodded. "Great, but if we're going out to lunch, I shouldn't stuff myself."

"You feel up to it, baby? Maybe you ought to stay in and rest today."

"And miss lunch at Yellowfinger's? No way!"

She took one last spoonful of oatmeal before putting the tray aside. He went to get dressed. She got up, plugged in her phone, and was about to dial Brad's number when it rang, scaring her out of her socks.

"County Morgue. Head stiff speaking!" she said.

"When's the funeral?" Brad inquired.

"Sorry, sir. You just missed it, but if you want to view the body, it'll be on display from six till eight this evening."

"You bet I want to view the body! It just happens to be my favorite body in the world. Did the doctor show up?" he asked.

"Yup! Right now she is probably out dining at some posh Beverly Hills bistro, eating up my father's hard-earned thirty bucks," Kim said.

"Thirty bucks for a housecall? Maybe I should think about becoming a doctor instead of a starving actor. So, what'd she say is wrong with you?" Brad asked anxiously.

"You ready for this? I have a sunburn."

"Hot news!"

"*Very*. I have to go to her office tomorrow morning. She wants to do some tests. Maybe she'll find out I'm suffering from some rare disease, something fascinating with a big, long name," Kim fantasized.

"There you go again. Imaginationitis," he laughed. "Listen, I'm coming over, okay?"

"You mean now?" asked Kim.

"No, like tomorrow. Sure now. When else?"

"I'm going out to lunch with my father," she reminded him.

"Oh! The usual Sunday bit."

"Right!"

"How about after that?" he continued.

"After that I'm going to study. The SATs, remember?" Kim had almost forgotten them herself. "Um, about last night. I'm sorry. I acted like a real *dork*. I don't know what came over me, I mean it."

"What are you talking about? You, a *dork*? Never!" He hesitated an instant, then added, "A *nerd*? Maybe. A *creep*? Sometimes. But never a *dork*."

"You're not mad at me?" Kim queried.

"For what, getting sick? Now you *are* being a *dork*. Listen, next time you go to the beach, make sure you go with me, not Jodi Birdbrain. I'll take care of you, make sure you don't stay in the sun too long," he reprimanded.

"Yes, Daddy!" she responded.

"I was worried about you. I'm glad you're okay. You sound much, uh, better. By the way, I love you!" he said.

"I love *you*!" Kim countered.

"Not as much as I love you."

"No, more."

Things were back to normal. It had been awhile since they'd been this relaxed together. Kim knew it was her fault. She heard the doorbell ring. A moment later she heard Jan talking to someone downstairs. The voice sounded familiar. Footsteps came up the stairs, and Mr. Sanders loomed in her doorway looking very ill-at-ease and silly in hiking shorts, a rugby shirt, and tennis shoes.

"Someone's here. I've got to hang up. Call you back, okay?" she said into the phone and hung up before Brad could respond. She looked up at Mr. Sanders and said, "Well, fancy meeting *you* here? To what do I owe the honor, if you don't mind my asking?" She loved people dropping in on her unannounced, especially when she looked like the Wreck of the *Hesperus* wearing her pajamas, ugly ones with teddy bears all over them. She tried to act blasé, unconcerned, as though people dropping in when she was in a state of semi-undress was no big deal. Good thing she had the sunburn, or he'd notice how she was blushing.

"I was worried about you. Jodi said you were sick," Sanders said, taking a tentative step toward her.

"I wasn't sick. Just had a sunburn. *Have* a sunburn, I mean, only it doesn't feel all that bad anymore."

"Oh! I got the impression it was something else. I'm relieved," he said and tried to smile. "So, uh, you still mad at me?"

"What do *you* think?" Kim asked

"I think you're still mad at me."

"Very insightful of you," she said.

"Kim, I was only doing what I thought was right. Don't you think I'd rather have you in the part of Kate than anyone? No one else is going to be able to play it the way you would. For the sake of the production, I'd be crazy not to cast you," he cajoled her.

"Then why didn't you?" she said.

He sighed. "I told you why. I *do* have a responsibility as a teacher, you know. The production isn't first and foremost. My students, and their needs and welfare, are. I would have felt guilty if I'd cast you in the part, as if I were taking advantage of you, burdening you beyond your capabilities. You're able to do an awful lot, Kim. More than almost anyone else in the group. But there's a limit to how much even *you* can deal with. I never would have forgiven myself if I'd given you the part, and you'd wound up getting sick or . . . or something."

"By *or something* what exactly do you mean, Mr. Sanders?" Kim asked, as if she didn't already know. He stammered something about her emotional state being every bit as important as her physical one. She said, "Look, you don't have to explain anything to *me*. You're the teacher, remember? The person in authority. Whatever you say goes. You made your decision. I have to abide by it. So, that's that."

"That's not fair," he said unhappily.

"We're friends, not just teacher and student. Your feelings are very important to me, Kim."

"Is that so? If they *were*, you wouldn't be doing this in the first place," she said coolly, looking down her nose at him.

He colored slightly and murmured, "I'm sorry you feel that way, but you'll see. A while from now you'll look back on this and realize it isn't the tragedy you think it is." He began to tell her how proud of her he was; how much she had accomplished in the past few years, as a performer, as a student, as a person; how she had grown and developed as an actress; and what a wonderful future she had to look forward to. He spoke wistfully, perhaps even with a touch of envy, because, after all, she *was* going to have the future he wished he could have had, and that must make him remorseful and sad. She felt sorry for him, and that made her angry at herself. Why should she feel sorry for *him*? He didn't deserve her sympathy. Not after what he had done. He sounded so sincere, though. Could she have been wrong about his reason for not giving her the part?

"Well, I have to go," he said,

"Thanks for stopping by. I really appreciate it," she said in a hoarse voice, keeping her eyes averted.

"Friends?" he asked in a hopeful tone.

She looked up at him. "Friends," she replied a little tentatively and forced herself to smile.

Seventeen

"I have saved you your usual table," monsieur, Pierre, the *maitre d'* at Yellowfinger's said to her father, ushering them to a table by the window.

"*Merci mille fois, Pierre,*" her father said in impeccable French and proceeded to dazzle everyone in the near vicinity by carrying on a lengthy conversation with Pierre, all in rapid-fire French. The waitress came to take their order. Kim ordered eggs benedict, her father a spinach salad. Sam and Pierre were still talking when the waitress brought the food. Kim stared at her plate. Why had she ordered eggs benedict? She didn't want eggs benedict. Just the thought of eating them turned her stomach. She speared one of the eggs with her fork, piercing the yolk so that it oozed out over the muffin.

"What's wrong?" her father asked, watching her.

"Oh, nothing." She forced herself to take a bite. She had a little difficulty chewing and swallowing it.

"You sure you're okay?"

"Sure. Fine, Daddy. It's the sunburn. It's making me feel weird."

"You *could* have a touch of sun poisoning."

"Not *that* weird!" She put her hand to her head. It was beginning to hurt again.

"We shouldn't have come," he said.

"No, I'm okay. Really. Now I know why people are always saying you should wear a hat when you sit out in the sun."

"Another headache, baby?"

"Just a little one, Daddy."

"Jan's right. You *are* getting a lot of them lately," Sam said.

"Mom got headaches. She got them all the time," she ventured.

"Mom *thought* she got headaches. Do you want to order something else?"

"No. This is fine," she said and forced in another mouthful. The feel of the yolk on her tongue made her shudder involuntarily.

"Jan's right about another thing. You're doing too much. That's why you're overtired. We've got to do something about that, baby, find a way for you to get the rest you need, cut back on some things."

She looked up from her plate. "On what, Daddy? If you can think of something I can cut back on, you're a lot smarter than *I* am. Believe me, I can't cut back on anything. I'm committed, up to my eyeballs, in fact. You know what you're always telling me, that once you take on a job, it's your responsibility? Well, I may have taken on too much, but it's too late to do anything about it now. I've got to see it all through, one way or the other."

"Of course. I see your point. Well, you *could* cut back on social things," he offered. She almost laughed. Social things? *What* social things? She didn't have any, other than Brad, and they didn't spend half enough time together as it was. If they saw each other any less, they wouldn't be seeing each other at all.

"Brad'll understand if he really cares about you and has your well-being in mind," her father said, pouring more dressing on his salad. She stared at him. *If?* Was the subtle message behind the comment that Brad really *didn't* care about her well-being?

No, wait. This was her father, not a disinterested party. He loved her and knew everything there was to know about her, didn't he? He had always been there for her, even when no one else had, and up until now he had usually given her the right advice, guided her in the right direction. Everything he wanted for her was exactly what she wanted for herself, and yet . . . and yet lately there were times when she felt he was wrong. Why couldn't she tell him so? You could still love a person and disagree with them, couldn't you? He *was* capable of being wrong, wasn't he? He wasn't God. On the other hand,

after all he had done for her, the sacrifices
he had made on her behalf, she owed him
something. She ought to try and do what
he asked, what he thought was right. He *was*
her father.

"Think about what I said," he advised
when they got home. "You'll see I'm right.
It's the only way, baby. What other options
do you have?"

*E*ighteen

"My father thinks the only way I can get through the rest of the school year is to stop going out so much," she said to Jodi later.

Jodi kicked off her shoes and flopped down on her bed. "So much? You hardly go out at all these days."

"Well, there's no way I can cut back on anything else, so that's it," Kim said finally.

Jodi gave her a long look and said, "Okay, if you say so, but you know how *I* feel on the subject. Listen, you're a big girl. You don't need *me* to tell you what to do . . . or your daddy either," she added meaningfully. "So, you don't need me to pick you up tomorrow morning?" she said, changing the subject.

Kim shook her head. "I have to go to the doctor. Jan's taking me. Then she'll drive me to school after that. I just hope I make it in time for the math test."

Jodi put a record on. Bob Seger's voice

thundered through the house. The phone rang. Kim pounced on it. "Turn it down, will you?" she shouted at Jodi, who raised the volume, then began to dance around the room.

"You having a party?" Brad asked.

"Jodi's having one, all by herself," Kim replied.

"You were supposed to call me back."

"Oh, my gosh! Brad, I forgot. Jeez, I must be getting senile, I mean it. I'm so absent-minded lately."

"That's all right. I've only been sitting here staring at the phone for three hours," he said.

"I got shook because Sanders walked in here, and after that, well, it was a highly dramatic scene, take my word."

"What'd *he* want?"

"To apologize to me. Oh, and explain his decision. Rather rationalize it. Oh, I don't know which. If that was an act he was putting on, it sure was terrific."

Jodi was really getting down. She boogied around the room, eyes closed, singing along with Bob.

Kim grinned at her. "Would you mind? I happen to be on the phone."

Jodi opened her eyes. "Was Sanders really here?"

"Eavesdropper!"

"Who, *me*?" Brad said in an injured tone.

"No, Jodi, Miss Disco of the Year."

Jodi did a nifty little step, snapping her fingers in time to the music. "Oooh, I love that man!" she sang, meaning Bob Seger, Kim supposed, not Sheldon Sanders.

"Why don't you take a break later, and we'll go out for a while?" Brad was saying.

"I can't. I'll probably be up half the night going over those notes, anyway," Kim replied, watching Jodi get down. "Don't tempt me. My resolve's shaky enough as it *is*. I've got to ace those SATs. My whole future depends on it."

"Compulsive-obsessive behavior," she heard Jodi mutter.

Later that day Kim had difficulty studying. Her powers of concentration were usually operating at peak level, but today they kept slipping away from her. It took all her determination to force herself to focus on her notes, which were copious. As Jan said, no one took more extensive, or thorough, notes than she did. She took more than she needed to really, but better more than less, as her father was always saying. Better to be over-prepared than under.

"Take a break and have some dinner," Jan cajoled at around seven.

"In a while," Kim murmured and went back to her notes. Fifteen minutes later Jan appeared with a tray. Without a word she set it down on the desk and went away. "You're unreal!" Kim called after her, feeling guilty. She should have gone down for dinner and not put Jan to all this trouble. She hadn't known how hungry she was until she started eating. Jan was a good cook. The chicken was delicious, and Jan had made her favorite vegetable, broccoli with cheese sauce, plus brown rice and a salad. *I can't possibly eat all this*, Kim thought, then proceeded to clean her plate. "Remind me to return the favor," she said to Jan when she came to take the tray away and bring her a mug of tea. "Next weekend you get breakfast in bed, both days, I promise!"

"How's it going?" Jan asked.

"Okay, but I've still got hours more to do," Kim replied.

"Don't stay up too late. Remember, you have to be at the doctor's at nine."

"Lord, I almost forgot! Couldn't we skip it? Really, there's nothing wrong with me, other than the sunburn, and that's all better, so I really don't need to go."

"You're going!" Jan said resolutely. Kim knew better than to argue. Once Jan made up her mind about something, it was useless to try and change it.

"You're one tough lady," Kim teased, smiling at her over the rim of her mug. "It's like living under the same roof with a drill sergeant."

"I'm taking my aggressions out on you, poor girl," Jan laughed, then said in a more serious tone, "I think it must be my innate maternal instinct working overtime. I'd probably be a terrible mother. Overzealous, overprotective, and overbearing."

"You'd probably be a terrific mother. Over-caring, overloving, overwonderful," Kim told her.

"I'm not about to get a chance to find out," Jan said a trifle regretfully.

"You *could*, though," Kim ventured hesitantly, then thought, *I shouldn't have said that.*

"Your father doesn't want any more children," Jan reminded her.

"I know, but what about what *you* want?" Kim couldn't help asking.

"We'd *both* have to want it," Jan replied.

"Maybe you should adopt. Think of all those kids out there, who don't have anybody, who are just waiting for you to come along and mother them to smithereens. You might even wind up saving a life; a couple of lives. If you're going to adopt, you ought to take two, not just one, don't you think?"

She was doing it again, writing a scene, visualizing Jan surrounded by kids of every description — big ones, little ones, one of every color and ethnic origin — sitting in a rocker (with a tiny baby on her lap) like in an old tintype photograph from bygone days.

Jan smiled and said, "I knew when your father and I got married how he felt. I'd never try to change his mind now. That wouldn't be fair — to him, to me, and most especially to the children."

*N*ineteen

At a little before nine the next morning, they were in Dr. Freed's waiting room. Kim had a magazine open on her lap, but it was just a prop. She wasn't really reading it. Jan sat on the imitation leather couch beside her, oohing and aahing over the latest copy of *Vogue*. Kim couldn't work up much enthusiasm for this season's latest fashions. She had other, more pressing, things on her mind. What was she doing here? Why did Dr. Freed think it was necessary to do these mysterious blood tests? What were those tests going to reveal about the state of her health?

There were two other people in the waiting room, a very large lady with a bad case of asthma and a little bald-headed man with the sniffles. A starched white nurse came and led Kim to a white, sterile examination room. She told Kim to get undressed and put on a white paper hospital gown, a nifty little number that barely tied in the back. The nurse said Dr. Freed would be right in, but she didn't show up until nearly half an hour later. By that time Kim was about to jump out of her skin. All she could think of was how late she was going to be for her math test. Maybe she wouldn't get there at all.

"You're the first person I've ever seen look good in one of those things," the doctor said, indicating the hospital gown.

"Chic little number, isn't it?" Kim replied, remembering to smile. Her face felt frozen. Dr. Freed had picked up a large, and very evil-looking, hypodermic needle and was advancing toward her with it. Kim had always been terrified of needles, ever since she was little, and this one was the biggest one she had ever seen. Next to needles, she hated the sight of blood — anybody's, but especially her own. As if she were mesmerized, she watched the needle enter the soft skin of her forearm, then fill with blood, *her* blood, her *precious* blood, the blood she resented having to part with, even one little drop of it.

"Your stepmother tells me you're under an unusual amount of stress lately," Dr. Freed said in a conversational tone and extracted the needle from her forearm.

Kim held on for dear life. "I'm always under stress. That's nothing new. It doesn't bother me," she said in somebody else's voice.

"It must on *some* level," the doctor pointed out, transferring blood from the syringe into a little glass vial, then another and another.

Kim watched, fascinated, as the doctor capped each vial with a little rubber stopper, then set it into a slotted glass holder. "You mean an unconscious one? Now you sound like my psych teacher, Ms. Horikawa. She's always saying all this stuff about unconscious feelings and reactions."

"As I said, it has to affect you some way, and, no matter how you look at it, it can't be beneficial."

Kim shrugged. "It's just part of my overall life-style; something I've gotten used to. I don't even notice it anymore."

"You don't *think* you do," the doctor said knowingly. Kim felt like slugging her. Did she always have to be so patronizing, such a know-it-all? Just because she happened to be a doctor didn't mean she knew everything.

"Is this going to take very long? I have a math exam, and I can't miss it," she muttered.

"What time is the exam?"

"Eleven-thirty."

"You'll make it."

"Well, that's something, anyway." Kim cringed as the doctor's little silver hammer connected with her kneecap. "You think I'm crazy or something?"

"No. Why do you ask?"

"I thought that was a test to find out if a person's got weird reactions."

"You were misinformed," Dr. Freed said with a smile and, taking a blood pressure apparatus from the cabinet, proceeded to test her blood pressure. The examination was very thorough. Kim hadn't expected it to be *this* thorough. She had thought the doctor was just going to be doing blood tests, but, as it turned out, no portion of her anatomy escaped the doctor's intense scrutiny, not even her heart and lungs. A nurse came and took her into an X-ray room for a chest X ray. Another one gave her an electrocardiogram, attaching all kinds of wires to different parts of her body, wires that hooked up to an EKG machine and measured her heart rate. After that came a stress test. Kim had to walk, then jog, on a motorized track that kept on moving faster and faster until she was running as fast as she could. Meanwhile a meter on the wall above her monitored her heart and pulse rates.

"When will you get back the test results?" she asked Dr. Freed when she was leaving.

"I'll call you," the doctor replied. "It should be in a few days."

"I can't wait!" Kim muttered. "Uh, listen, Doc, as far as you could see from what you did right now — without the test results, that is — what do you think's the matter with me?"

"Are you worried?" the doctor asked.

"Worried? No, well, I just wouldn't like any surprises, like to suddenly find out I've got some dread terminal disease," Kim joked.

"Is that what you think?" he asked.

"The thought *had* crossed my mind," Kim replied.

"There's not the slightest chance of anything like that. Does that answer your question?"

"Yes, as a matter of fact, it *does*." Kim followed Jan out the door. "I guess, if Dr. Freed's willing to put herself on the line and tell me that, I'm really *not* suffering from something all that drastic."

Jan looked at her. "You really *were* worried."

"Not really worried, but wondering. People don't walk around feeling cruddy for no reason, do they? Listen, thanks for coming with me. I hate going to the doctor."

"Me, too. Next time I have to go, you can accompany *me*."

"A deal! Man, am I ever glad Dad got lucky and found *you*. Every day I say a little prayer of thanks to Cupid for arranging it. Know what I really love about you? I mean, in addition to all kinds of other things. You're so totally upfront and honest. I always know, when you say something, you really mean it, not a whole bunch of other things. You never con me. You don't know how much I appreciate that. Remember what you said to me the other day, about my opening up and letting my real self out? Um, well, I was wondering. How do you let your real self out if you don't know who that *is*? It's very confusing. I'm trying to locate the real Kim Stanton, but she's a little elusive."

"All I meant was that you shouldn't pretend to feel something you really don't, that you ought to feel free to express your feelings about things, that's all," Jan explained.

"You mean like when somebody does something to me, and I don't like it, instead of pretending I don't mind, I should tell them?"

"Yes, that's part of it."

"And if someone wants one thing, and I want another, I should say what I want instead of doing it their way all the time, being so accommodating."

"That, too."

"Oh! I thought you meant I was two different people, the person I really am inside and the one everyone else thinks I am. Something like that."

"Very few of us go around displaying our innermost feelings to the outside world on a steady basis," Jan said. "In a way we're all two people."

"My psych teacher's always saying that. When you said that the other day, I thought you were thinking I was neurotic, like a split personality or something."

"Neurotic? No. Just human. That's just it," Jan added, putting a hand on top of hers. "I want you to know you're allowed to be."

"Who says I don't?" Kim said a trifle defensively.

"No one, only, well, sometimes I think you feel you have to be this superperson. It's quite a strain walking around being perfect all the time."

"You think I do that?"

"I think you think you should."

"Maybe you're right. Miss Perfect, that's what they call me at school; the girl who has everything, and does everything, better than anybody. They think it comes easy, that I don't even have to make an effort to be super-good at everything. If they only knew how hard it is, they'd be shocked. I guess that's what you mean, isn't it? Like Jodi's always saying, I've got this problem. I think I have to be Number One, the best at everything, a winner all the time, and if I'm not, I see myself as a big, fat failure."

"Sounds like someone else I know," Jan murmured.

"You mean Daddy?"

"You two *are* alike in that way."

"A lot of other ways, too."

Jan nodded. "I just want you to realize that you can't devote your whole life to being what someone else wants you to be. It's what *you* want that's important. You only have to be true to yourself, Kim, no one else."

Jan pulled up in front of the school. Kim leaned over and kissed her. "I love you a lot!" she said and climbed out of the car.

"Love you, too!" Jan called after her as she pulled away. Kim couldn't help thinking of something her mother had once said to her. It hadn't meant all that much to her at the time her mother said it, but it sure did now. *"You can't go through life trying to live up to someone else's expectations. All you can do is live up to your own, be your own person, the person you really want to be."*

Twenty

Kim checked out the clock over the main doors. Eleven-ten. She still had time. She ran past the auditorium. A piece of paper was tacked up on the bulletin board outside the double doors. There it was in black and white, the list of the cast for *Kiss Me, Kate!* The letters seemed to grow larger and darker before her eyes as she stood there staring at them:

PETRUCHIO — Ben Hernandez

VINCENTIO — Scott Osborne

LUCENTIO — Lance Greenberg

GREMIO — B. J. Burnside

HORTENSIO — Todd Chew

KATE — Linda Flores

BIANCA — Margie Kaplow

It hurt to see someone else's name up there. Given the options, she supposed Linda was the logical choice. Why did she feel as though someone had just punched her in the *solar plexus*? It wasn't as though she hadn't already known, or had she been expecting Sanders to change his mind, issue a last-minute reprieve, and put her in the part after all, for the good of the show? That only happened in 1940's movies with Judy Garland and Mickey Rooney. Never in real life.

"Did you see the notice?" Jodi asked when Kim got to class.

"Yeah. I saw it." She followed Jodi into the classroom. Scott Osborne reached over and tapped her on the shoulder.

"Hey, Chief baby, meet me in the newspaper office right after class. Something I have to check out with you."

"Dammit, will you please stop calling me Chief baby?" she snapped at him. "Sorry," she mumbled, guilty because she was in a bad mood and had taken it out on him.

"What happened at the doctor's?" Jodi asked.

"Nothing. She's doing some tests. I won't know the results for a while, but she says I'm going to live. I don't know whether that's good news or bad. Frankly, at this point, I don't think I want to."

Ms. Popkin came in and started handing out test papers. Kim looked at the first example on the sheet and panicked. It hadn't been on their study sheet. Popkin had thrown them a curve. *Typical! Okay, don't choke. It's only one example. What about the rest? What a relief!* Kim sighed. They were all similar to the examples on the sheet. Even if she missed the first one, if she got all the others right, she still had her A.

"How do you think you did?" Jodi asked when they were leaving the classroom.

"I think I aced it. How about you?"

"I think I flunked it. Oh, well, you win a few; you lose a few. That's life."

"Jodi, you couldn't have flunked it. You *did* study, didn't you?"

"In a way."

"What way?" Kim persisted.

"Tony came over. We watched a movie on the tube and . . . oh, never mind. Even if I study for weeks, I don't do all that well. I've *got* to pass the course, or I'll wind up in summer school."

Kim hurried to the newspaper office. Scott was at the drawing board working on the cartoon. Kim peered over his shoulder. A girl who looked suspiciously like Jodi, wearing the shortest skirt imaginable, was walking past the principal's office, being ogled by a group of guys who looked like Ben Hernandez, Lance Greenberg, Billy Raines, Todd Chew, and Scott himself. A man wearing a T-shirt with MR. BIG on the front, who bore a striking resemblance to Mr. Biggar, wig and all, was watching them from behind the door of the office, or rather leering at the girl. Underneath the cartoon was the caption, "Bending the Rules."

"I don't know whether we'll get it past Biggy. You'd better have a backup ready in case," she said, checking out the Work Completed box to see if anyone had done anything they were supposed to do. Of course not. Had she expected them to? Other than Kim and Scott, no one on the staff did any work. They left it all up to her, even the photographs. Why not? They all knew she would rise to the occasion. If she was nothing else, she was predictable.

Where would she find the time? She was so far behind as it was. What if she *had* played Kate? How would she have managed it? She hated having to admit it, even to herself, but Sanders had been right. She would have wound up in deep trouble, maybe even blown the whole thing. There was no way she would have been able to do it and all these other things, too. No way in the world.

She hurried to English, praying that Marshbanks wasn't going to be in one of his long-winded moods. She didn't think she was up for one of his two-hour lectures, especially on Thomas Hardy. Her head was killing her. Another headache in the life of Kimberly Stanton, soap opera heroine, the girl who had more problems than any six other soap opera heroines put together. *Go away*, she told the headache, but it was getting worse and worse. She thought of what her father always said about her mother's headaches, that they were imaginary, psychological. Were hers psychological, too? If so, she was in a bad way.

Marshbanks *was* in a long-winded mood. *Tess of the D'Urbervilles* was not one of

Kim's favorite pieces of fiction. She tried to focus on what he was saying, but her mind kept wandering. What was Brad doing right now? Was he thinking about her? This really *was* the longest class in history. She would be a basket case by the time it ended.

Marshbanks concluded his lecture on *Tess* by exhorting the class to read the novel in its entirety, not rely on the published notes to get them through the exam. He was fanatical in his belief that being well-read was the next most important thing in life to being toilet-trained. Of course three-quarters of the kids would ignore his advice and cop out by reading the notes. Kim wouldn't be one of them. It would have been nice to find a shortcut just once in her life, instead of doing everything the long way — the *right* way, she reminded herself. Unfortunately, it just wasn't in her to take shortcuts.

Margie was at the usual stand in the cafeteria eating lunch. "You look great! Did you go to the beach over the weekend?" she asked between mouthfuls.

"I'm trying not to think about it." Kim collapsed into a chair.

"Don't you ever eat?" Margie asked.

"Once a year," Kim replied.

"I wrote the speech," Margie said and waited for Kim to offer congratulations.

Kim got out a pencil instead and said, "Then let's get to work." Margie rummaged in her book bag and came up with a crinkled-up, messy sheaf of notebook pages with scribbling all over them. She handed them to Kim, who looked them over before saying, "I'd have to be a decoding expert to decipher this. You really expect anybody to be able to *read* this? It's illegible! The least you could've done was write legibly, Margie."

"I'm sorry. I was in a hurry. I did it during English, and Marshbanks had his evil eye on me. I pretended I was taking notes, but I don't think he believed it."

"You waited until last period to do this? My God, Margie, you really have some nerve! I mean, I'm giving up my precious time — and it *is* precious to me, for your information, what there *is* of it — to help you, and you can't even take the time and make the effort to do a halfway-decent job. It's *your* speech, not mine. I shouldn't even be helping you."

"Look, I'm not good at this sort of thing," Margie explained. "I never *was* much good at writing things or making speeches. I even flunked my P.E. presentation. I didn't want to join the stupid debating team to begin with. It was my parents' idea, not mine. See, they think it'll look good on my record, and that'll help me get into a better college. Listen, I can use all the help I can get. My grades are pretty bad. They're really gung ho about my going to college. They're always nudging me to bring up my grades, join things and stuff. If they had *you* for a kid, they'd be ecstatic, but I'm not into school. I wouldn't even *go* to college if they didn't make me. I do all this stuff to shut them up, so they won't hassle me. I wouldn't otherwise."

For a girl who claimed not to be all that good at speechmaking, Margie had done a pretty fair job on delivering *that* speech, Kim thought. She was sorely tempted to tell Margie just what she could do with her speech, but instead she spread the pages out on the table and started going over them, line by line, penciling in comments, questions and suggestions for revision.

"You'll have to do a major rewrite. This isn't even really a speech, Margie."

"A rewrite? You want *me* to do a rewrite? I had enough trouble doing *this*. I never rewrite anything I write. I can't. Look, why don't *you* rewrite it for me?"

"Why don't I *what*?"

"Rewrite it for me. If *I* do it, it could wind up losing us the finals. You don't want that to happen, do you, Kim? I mean, I know how important winning is to you and all. . . ."

Very deliberately Kim put the pages in their proper order, making sure they were perfectly aligned. Then she put them down on top of Margie's plate of turkey tettrazini, gathered her things, and stood up. "I like winning, but not *that* much," she said and smiled angelically at the other girl. "As a friend of mine is always saying, 'You win a few; you lose a few.' That's life!" And with that she marched out of the cafeteria, her resolve diminishing with every step she took. What was happening to her? Why had she done that? Where was Miss Perfect now?

*T*wenty·one

"You're a mirage, a figment of my imagination. You're not really here. I just *think* you are," Jodi said and started staggering around the parking lot in a deranged state.

"Let's just say turkey tettrazini isn't one of my favorite dishes," Kim laughed, following her to the car.

"Well, my dear, you'll never guess who showed up at the restaurant during my shift last night. I'll give you a little hint. His initials are B.E.B., and he has the prettiest legs in the San Fernando Valley." Jodi headed Sidney toward Fat City.

"*You* have the prettiest legs in the San Fernando Valley," Kim pointed out.

"True. His are second-prettiest," Jodi said.

"Why didn't you tell me before?"

"Guess I forgot." Jodi started murmuring sweet nothings to Sidney, hoping to deter him from staging a revolt. "By the way, why weren't you with him?" she asked Kim.

"You know why. I was home studying for the SATs."

"Where else? So, have you told him about your father's idea?"

"No. Listen, could we talk about something else? I have a feeling I'm going to be sorry I didn't stay in the cafeteria and eat turkey tettrazini."

"Far be it for me to interfere," Jodi said, and pulled out of the parking space, "but you don't know Brad as well as you think you do. He's really not secure and bursting with self-confidence."

"Jodi, Brad happens to be the most secure, confident person in the world. If you were thinking of making psychology your life's work, forget it. It's not your forté."

"Just trying to help," Jodi said.

"I know, and I appreciate the sentiment, but you're a little misguided," Kim said. At Fat City she watched Jodi consume her favorite sandwich, peanut butter and banana, plus a vanilla shake.

"Aren't you eating?" Jodi asked.

"Lost my appetite," Kim replied. "I'll have something later."

"Your eyes look funny. Got another headache?"

"No," Kim lied. "I feel fine."

"Okay, if you say so," Jodi said, acting offended, and went back to her food.

They got back to school early. Kim headed for the library to check out some books she needed for her English report. She was passing the auditorium when she heard voices coming from inside, or rather *one* voice, Mr. Sanders'. She opened the door and slipped inside to listen. He and the cast and crew were up on the stage, and he was delivering his usual pre-productional pep talk, the same one he delivered to the cast and crew before every production, almost word-for-word. By this time she knew it by heart.

"People, this isn't just any high school. It's Montebello. We're not just any drama club. We're the Thespians, the best amateur high school group in southern California. We didn't get to be the best the easy way. It took plenty of hard work, *teamwork*. Talent isn't enough. You've got to have devotion and dedication to make it in *this* business. You've got to have guts. You've got to be willing to make sacrifices, lots of them. . . ."

Oh, sure. Devotion. Dedication. Sacrifice. Where had they gotten her? Nowhere. Out on her rump, standing in the back of the auditorium watching somebody else play her part. She slipped back out the door and hurried down the corridor. Scott Osborne came out of the newspaper office.

"Chief baby, just the person I wanted to see," he said, linking arms with her, and zapped her with the news that Biggy wanted the newspaper staff to get out an extra edition of the paper, a centennial edition, Scott called it.

"Oh, no!" she groaned, on the verge of

136

tears. He looked at her as though he thought she was overreacting. She tried to explain. "It's just that I'm swamped as it *is*, and . . . oh, never mind! We'll have to manage. I *could* use some help. You're the only one who bothers."

He started singing "Happy Birthday" to the school. She joined in on the chorus. Outside psych they met Linda Flores. Kim smiled through clenched teeth. She ought to say something gracious to show she was a good sport and not a sore loser. How about something like, *"Hey, Linda, I can't wait till opening night. I want to be out there in the audience when you get up on that stage in front of all those people and make a total and complete idiot of yourself."* Or, *"Hey, Linda baby, break a leg. Break two. Three. All four of them. Woof, woof!"*

"Congratulations, Linda, I know you'll be wonderful in the part!" she said with warmth and sincerity.

Jodi appeared out of nowhere and whispered in her ear, "Very convincing. You're a great actress, you know it?"

Kim spun around, startled. "Cool it, Adams! You're always creeping up on me."

"Me? I don't creep. I stride. I stalk. I saunter. Sometimes I even sashay, but I never creep!" Jodi declared. Then, right in front of everybody, she got down on all fours and crawled into the classroom. Kim didn't change expression. She just walked in after her, acting as though it was the most natural thing in the world to enter a classroom behind a person on all fours.

"What time do you have to be at work?" she asked.

"Why?" Jodi crawled into her seat.

"I was thinking maybe we could go to the mall. I saw this adorable stuffed dog I want to get for Brad for Valentine's Day."

"A stuffed animal for a guy?"

"Why not?"

"You're right. Why not? We're liberated! I switched with one of the other waitresses, so I don't have to go till later. It's pretty out of character, you wanting to go somewhere after school, except to your lesson or home to do your homework. You turning over a new leaf?" Jodi asked.

"Taking your advice. All work and no play, remember? So, you want to go, or not?" said Kim.

"Yeah, sure. I can get something for Tony. I haven't bought him anything yet."

Kim forced a smile and tried to convince herself that she really did want to go shopping. For the next two hours she wasn't going to think about Margie's speech, the newspaper, or any of her responsibilities. She was just going to relax; that is, if she still knew how.

There was a big sale at Marshall's. Jodi lucked out and got six pairs of panty hose for the price of three. To celebrate saving all that money, she treated herself to three pairs of outrageous designer knee socks and a red patent leather waist-cincher belt, at half price. They browsed for awhile, then went to Orient Express so Jodi could have an eggroll. After that they went to the toy store where Kim had seen the stuffed English sheepdog she wanted to buy for Brad, only they were all out of stuffed English sheepdogs, so she had to settle for a stuffed Lhasa apso instead.

"I don't know why you're upset. A dog's a dog," Jodi said when they were leaving.

"Eustace happens to be an English sheepdog, not a Lhasa apso," Kim explained.

"So, Brad won't call it Eustace. He'll call it something else, something more appropriate, like Sheldon, for instance. It looks like a Sheldon, don't you think? Those big, brown soulful eyes? Brad can take it to bed with him, along with his bankie, his teddy, and his pacifier. It can keep him company when he gets lonely, which is probably all the time lately. *You*, of course, are far too concerned with earth-shaking matters of importance to fritter away your time dallying with one inconsequential boyfriend."

"I knew it was too good to last," Kim muttered to herself, tucking Sheldon under her arm. "Come on. I'll be late for my lesson."

"Ah, the dahnce!" Jodi cried and started pirouetting around in front of the Orange Julius stand, watched by a throng of people and one lovesick boy in an Orange Julius hat and apron who got so carried away watching her that he spilled a whole blender-full of the drink all over a customer.

Twenty-two

Madame Bartova's École de Ballet, a run-down, seedy building at the wrong end of town, was two doors away from the freeway. It was two flights up to a studio that looked as though it hadn't been painted in two hundred years. It was even older than Madame, if such a thing was possible. Madame had to be the world's oldest living human being; a hundred if she was a day, reckoning by the stories she told of her younger years in Russia before the revolution. When she was a girl, she danced with Nijinsky and Diaghilev, the Ballet Rousse de Monte Carlo. Isadora Duncan had been one of her closest friends.

Madame was the harshest, toughest teacher on earth. She didn't let her students get away with a thing. Lessons from Madame meant working her leotard off, but Kim learned. Madame would never forgive Kim for deciding to be an actress instead of a ballet dancer. She saw it as a criminal act. At every opportunity she lectured her, trying to get her to change her mind.

Kim took her place at the ballet *barre* and started her warmup. She could hear her joints popping and creaking, her muscles rebelling as she forced them to stretch beyond their limits. Tiffany Levine came in, followed by four other girls. They went through the prescribed exercises, watching themselves in the mirrors. On the stroke of five, Madame made her entrance, a tiny woman wearing a one-piece black leotard to her ankles; her hair, dyed jet black, was in a chignon at the back of her neck, covered by a net. Her face was a mass of wrinkles. Her features just disappeared in wrinkles. But her body was young.

"Plié, plié, and lift, lift, lift!" Madame bellowed, beating the floor with her cane. "Tiffany, you are supposet to be a svan, a svan, not a baby elephant. Kimberly, you are a svan, not a robot. Vhat is wronk vit you today?"

"A little tired, Madame. Sorry!"

"Tired? You come here tired? Shame, shame on you! Aha, I see vat is wronk. You think you can fool *me*? You haff been skippink the vorkouts, yes?"

"Yes, Madame. I've been so busy, and . . ."

"No excuses, pleaze! The dance, it shouldt come first before everythink. If you cannot giff it your all, you shouldt not be here."

"You are right. I shouldn't," Kim muttered. Either Madame didn't hear her or she chose not to, because she didn't say anything else, except to bellow at them, "A svan, a svan. Plié, plié, lift, lift, lift! Ven I vass vith Nijinsky, he uset to say there vas not another dancer as light as I. Lighter than air. He usedt to say to me, 'Ah, Natasha Stanisalova, you are light as a feather!'"

Kim strained to get the movements exactly right. She was drenched with perspiration. It was pouring down her, soaking through the tights and leotard. She hurt. Every part of her hurt so bad she could hardly bear it, but she kept on going, refusing to give into herself, or to give Madame the satisfaction of seeing her quit when the going got rough. Her head was throbbing, the pain nearly blinding her, but still she kept on dancing. Madame knew. She knew everything. She knew from just looking at you when something was wrong, from the way you moved, the way you arched a foot or pointed a toe. "You haff a sore tendon in your lefdt legg, yess?" she would intone, pointing at the recalcitrant part of your anatomy with her cane. "There! Just there. Such a thingk vould not heppen if you vere doing it right." Kim glanced up at the clock on the wall. Time went so slowly when you wanted it to go fast. The lesson was interminable. If only it would end, and she could get out of here.

When it was at last over, she hurried to change and escaped down the stairs and into the street. Someone came pounding down the stairs after her.

"Plié, plié, and lift, lift, lift!" Tiffany cackled, she sounding precisely like Madame on a rampage.

Kim burst out laughing. "That's great! You really have an ear for voices. Ever think of being an actress?"

"*Me*? I'm not pretty enough."

"You could've fooled *me*. Listen, even if you weren't, which you *are*, actresses don't have to be raving beauties anymore. More emphasis is put on other, more important, things, like talent, training, um, who you know, what friends you happen to have in high places. Need a lift?" Kim asked turning in at the parking lot.

Tiffany shook her head. "My mom's picking me up. Why don't we get together sometime? We could go to a movie or something maybe."

"I'd like that, Tiffany. I'm a little busy right now, but . . ."

"Oh, hey, no sweat! I didn't mean tomorrow or anything," Tiffany said.

"I really *want* to. It's just that I'm up to my ears in work and stuff, but how about during Easter vacation?" Kim ventured.

"Terrific!" Tiffany said, beaming at her. "You sure you really want to?"

"I said so, didn't I? Listen, give me your number so, just in case we don't get a chance to set it up beforehand, I can call you," Kim said and got out her appointment book and a pen. Tiffany scribbled her phone number on a page near the back and handed it back to her. A station wagon pulled up to the curb.

"There's my mom. Gotta split. Don't forget you promised you'd call me," Tiffany said, taking off.

"Don't forget. Plié, plié, and lift, lift, lift!" Kim called after her. Easter vacation seemed light-years away. Who knew what kind of shape she'd be in by then? Maybe not even among the living if things kept going as they were now. *Nice, positive thinking, Stanton!* she thought, smiling wryly to herself. Somehow she'd have to find time to fit in a date with Tiffany. She liked Tiffany.

Twenty·three

She spotted the balloons when she was coming off the freeway, a huge bunch of pink and red balloons bobbing around in the sky about a half a mile away. They were in her neighborhood. Maybe the Jacksons' house. They were newlyweds, and those looked like Valentine's Day balloons. She turned onto Forest Drive, then Elm, then Cypress, and realized with a shock that the balloons were above *her* house, not the Jacksons'. A pre-Valentine's present? She got out of the car and took a closer look. They had messages on them, personalized ones: *"I LOVE YOU, KIM! B.E.B. LOVES K.A.S. FOREVER, BRAD!"* Brad's VW was parked in the driveway. He was sitting on the stoop in front of the kitchen door.

"If the mountain won't come to Mohammed . . . ," he started.

"Bradley E. Berson, you nut!" She fell into his arms. "You are certifiably crazy."

"So they keep telling me. So, happy pre-Valentine's Day. Some guy was selling them outside school. He only popped a dozen writing on them." He followed her into the house. "You doing anything right now, like composing Beethoven's Fifth, or writing the Gettysburg Address, the Odyssey, or the Iliad, because I was thinking we could go out to dinner. Play your cards right, I might even take you for Chinese food. Moo shu pork? Shrimp with snow peas? Spareribs? Fried rice? You're probably ravenous, anyway, after all that leaping around at Madame What's-Her-Name's."

"Spareribs. Shrimp with snow peas. Moo shu pork. Mmm," she murmured, imagining how they would taste. He squeezed her a little too hard, and she let out a squeak. "Oooh, be careful! My poor muscles are about to go out on strike. Madame, the slave driver, really socked it to me today. I hurt in places I didn't even know I had. She really let me have it for skipping that last lesson."

"After dinner we could come back here and neck a lot," he mused.

"Massage my back. I'm dying," she moaned, turning her back to him. "Right there! Ooch. Under my right shoulder blade. Aaaaah, that's the little bugger that always gets me." She felt his lips on the back of her neck and shivered involuntarily. "Mmm, that gives me goose bumps. *Yikes!* That hurts," she screeched when his fingers dug into a muscle.

"It's tension," Brad stated.

"No kidding!"

"Tension and frustration. Lack of love. You ought to spend a little more time with your boyfriend. He's crazy about you, and, besides, think of it as therapy," he went on, enjoying his prescription.

"Keep rubbing," she sighed, beginning to relax. "Shouldn't we bring the balloons inside?"

"I think they look kind of cute out there myself."

"Okay, we'll leave them there then. You do the most adorable things sometimes. *All* the time," she amended, closing her eyes and sagging against him.

"Are we going out to dinner? Say no, and I'll stop massaging you," he threatened.

She smiled. "What are you all of a sudden, a millionaire? Listen, why don't I cook something instead?" she suggested, beginning to purr. "Um, that feels *so* good! Jan and my father aren't coming home till late. I could make something *exotic*. I saw this neat recipe for eggplant parmigiana in the *Times'* food section. Why don't I make that?"

"You really feel like cooking?" he asked.

"Sure! Why not? You can assist," Kim answered.

Brad had another idea. "Let's neck first and eat later."

"I thought you were so hungry," Kim said.

"Right, but not for food!"

She got out a knife and handed it to him, then got the eggplant out of the refrigerator and put it down on the wooden chopping board. "Peel, please," she ordered and went to get the bread crumbs and the cheese. She got out the skillet, put it on the burner, and poured a little cooking oil on it. "You're so good to me, so understanding. I don't know what I did to deserve you," she murmured.

"You're right. I am pretty incredible." He finished peeling the eggplant and handed it to her. She cut it in slices, whipped up an egg, shook some bread crumbs onto a plate, and started dipping slices of eggplant, first in the egg, then in the bread crumbs. He watched her, fascinated.

"Listen, I made reservations at Antonio's for next Saturday night. A lot of the kids from school are going there after the dance. We have to be at Pauley Pavillion by noon. They're serving a buffet lunch before the game."

She went to get the sauce out of the pantry closet. "I wanted to talk to you about that."

"Are you going to tell me you can't go?" Brad said in a defensive voice.

"Would you be awfully upset if I skipped the game and just went to the dance?" she asked.

"How did I know you were going to say that?"

"I don't know. How *did* you? It's just that

I found out we're going to have to get out an extra edition of the paper, and with all this other stuff I have to do — Brad, please understand."

"Yeah, well, don't sweat it. I didn't really want to go, anyway," he said, interrupting her. "Funny how I knew you were going to do this. You're getting to be awfully predictable, you know it? Good thing I'm not the paranoid type, or I'd start to think you were trying to tell me something, like you don't feel the same as you used to."

She stared at him. "How can you say that?"

"Easy! How would *you* feel if you were in my place? Your skillet's about to burn," he added, turning away.

"I take it back. You're *not* very understanding," she murmured and turned off the burner.

"There's a limit to how understanding even *I* can be," he replied.

"You don't want to share me with anything or anyone. You want me all to yourself. You ought to go and find yourself a girl who hasn't got anything, or anyone, in her life but you. Then she can devote herself to you twenty-four hours a day every day of her life."

What on earth had made her say that? It was ridiculous, also totally untrue. He just stood there looking at her for a moment, his face expressionless. Then his eyes narrowed, and he said, "Is that what you think?"

No, of course it isn't! a voice inside her head replied, but she opened her mouth and said, "Yes, it *is!*"

"You know, that's not a half-bad idea you had," he informed her in an icy tone and headed for the door.

"Where are you going?" she asked.

"To do what you said, find myself a girl, one who has time for me," he replied and, without another word, without even glancing in her direction, he stalked out the door, slamming it behind him so hard the whole house shook.

Twenty-four

"What a day. I knew I should have taken a sick day and stayed home the minute I woke up this morning. Why didn't I?" Jan said, lunging into the kitchen.

"What's wrong?" Kim asked, rushing over to her.

"Oh, nothing. I just came dangerously close to being fired, lost a fat bonus from opening my fat mouth once too often, spilled coffee all over myself during my coffee break, had a fight with one of the secretaries, and got a flat tire."

"So, aside from all that, what else is new?" Kim said, putting an arm around her. "Let's have a cup of tea or something. Um, better still, why don't you have a drink, a good, stiff one. A martini maybe. That's stiff, isn't it?"

"It's not the martini that's stiff. It's *you* after you drink it," Jan sighed and fell into a chair. She stretched out her legs. "Oooh, my poor feet! I feel like the little mermaid in that fairy tale by Hans Christian Andersen."

Kim bent down to take off Jan's shoes. You guys going out tonight?"

"We were supposed to. How could I go anywhere with coffee stains all over me? Did I see Brad just now?"

"Umm," Kim responded.

"Anything wrong?"

"Umm," Kim said again.

"Don't con *me*. There is, isn't there?"

"Jan, please . . ."

"You cooking? Eggplant parmigiana?"

"I don't know what got into Brad," Kim said. "You should have seen him. He had a bona fide temper tantrum, and all because I said I might not be able to go to a basketball game with him. Jan, Brad detests basketball," Kim added and started massaging one foot.

"It could have something to do with the fact that you've been breaking dates with him on a pretty regular basis lately," Jan ventured, wriggling her toes in ecstasy. "That might be what's upsetting him."

"Who isn't upset about that, but I'm not doing it because I want to, because I'd rather sit here with my nose in a book than be with *him*. He knows that, doesn't he? If he doesn't, he's pretty dumb!"

"Maybe he thinks you have some other reason for breaking those dates," Jan said. Kim stared at her. Some other reason? What other reason could there possibly be? That she was secretly madly in love with another guy and seeing him on the sly? She gave Jan's toes one yank a piece to get the kinks out, then stood up. "Where are you going?" Jan asked when she headed for the door.

"I've got to think. Would you mind if I took off for a while?"

"Be my guest, but take it easy, will you?"

"Yeah, sure. Don't bother with this mess. I'll clean up the rest of it when I get back. I won't be long."

Sometimes a person needed to be alone and think. Jan was wonderful, the best, but right now was one of those times. She drove aimlessly with no particular destination in mind. It was rush hour. The traffic was pretty heavy, so she avoided the freeway. She passed the school and thought it would feel good to run, so she doubled back, pulled into the parking lot behind the building, got out of the car, and headed for the track. Someone was already there, running.

"Well, if it isn't Miss Perfect!" Billy Raines said when she caught up with him and gave her one of his famous you're-an-insect-and-I'm-insectivorous looks. She ignored him and kept on going. "Why aren't you in the auditorium rehearsing with the rest of the creeps?" he called after her.

"Because I'm out here on this track beating the pants off *you*, Billy Boy," she called back. He was fifteen pounds overweight, flabby, and out of shape. He wasn't giving her much competition. Ballerinas shouldn't run. Not if they could help it. Well, since she wasn't planning on being a ballerina, she would run if she felt like it, and she felt like it.

Jan and Jodi thought alike about some things. Two such entirely different people, yet they were in agreement. If your best friend and your stepmother, both of whom were devoted to you, thought the same thing, maybe they were right. At least you ought to take what they were saying under consideration.

Was she taking Brad for granted, being selfish and self-centered, only thinking of herself, her own needs and problems? He was so good to her, so understanding. He always let her have things her way. Maybe he was *too* good. And maybe, because he *was*, she took advantage of him.

So, here she was, sixteen, self-centered, self-involved, and self-defeating; overextended, overachieved, and definitely overwhelmed. Miss Perfect, the most messed up girl in the world. What was she going to do about it?

It was late. Jan would be worried about her. She wouldn't go out until Kim was safely home, tucked in for the night. It was a big responsibility having a stepmother who was that devoted to you. You had to watch your step or she got traumatized.

Kim left the track, jogged across the field

to the parking lot, and walked around for a moment to catch her breath. She got into the car, pulled out of the lot and took her usual route home — De Soto Street to Winnetka; Winnetka to Orange Road, then right on Fallbrook; right again on Penrose Alley, which brought her to Marathon, Canoga, and, finally, Ventura Boulevard, three blocks from home. She never saw the other car coming until it was too late. Suddenly there it was looming up before her, mere inches away. She rammed her foot down on the brake and came to a screeching, jarring, grinding stop half an inch away from its front left fender. It was an ominous-looking car, a big, black, shiny Cadillac. A man leaped out from behind the wheel and advanced toward her, screaming.

"Where did you learn to drive, you idiot? Kids!" he growled in a derogatory tone when he saw she was one. "You're all alike. No sense of responsibility. No consideration for anyone else. Only thinking of yourselves. Sure! It's *your* America. The hell with the rest of us." He went on berating her. She sat there at the wheel staring out the window at him.

"I'm s . . . so sorry!" she exclaimed when she could get a word in.

"Yeah, sure. Sorry. That's a stop sign, kid. You know what you do when you come to a stop sign?"

"You stop," she said in a small voice.

"Brilliant!" He took a closer look at her, and his face softened a little. "You okay, kid? You hurt or anything?"

"N . . . no. I'm not hurt," she said in a hoarse voice.

He held up his thumb and forefinger a half an inch apart. "That was close. You came that close to hitting me. Lucky!"

"I'm s . . . so sorry! Usually I'm such a careful driver. I've never even come *close* to having an accident," she stammered.

"Let me tell you something, Missy, I've been driving thirty years. When you drive *that* long, and you can say you've never had an accident, then you know you're a safe driver."

"It was all my fault," she ventured.

"You're damned right it was! You sure you're okay? You don't look right," he muttered, peering at her over the tops of his bifocals.

"I'm all right. Really," she hastened to assure him. "Do you want to take my name and phone number? I can show you my license and the car registration if you want to see them."

"No. Not necessary," he assured her, a lot friendlier now. "Look, just watch what you're doing from now on, young lady. Do yourself and everyone else a favor and keep your mind on your driving."

"I will. I promise." She watched him walk back to his car. If not for half an inch, she could be dead right now. Half an inch, that was all there had been between her and disaster, maybe even death. Knowing that gave her a whole new slant on things. She sorted out her priorities real quick. *"In Memorium. Miss Perfect, the girl most likely to succeed (if only she had lived long enough), but, alas, Miss Perfect is now pushing up the daisies, six feet underground."* She didn't think they were about to write on her tombstone, *"Here lies Kim Stanton, a.k.a. Miss Perfect. She always got straight A's."*

"Dr. Freed called. She wants us to come in tomorrow morning. The test results came back," Jan said when Kim walked in.

"Did anyone else call?" Kim asked.

"If you mean Brad, no," Jan replied.

"You cleaned up the kitchen. I told you I'd do it," Kim said guiltily.

Jan was looking at her oddly. She said, "Nothing much left to clean up. No problem. You okay? You look so pale."

"Are you leaving now, or what?"

"In a minute. Something happen I should know about?" Jan didn't give up easily.

"No, nothing. I went to the track. Ran a little. It felt good. Will you be home late?"

"No. Would you rather I didn't go? Your father could go without me. The other people would probably prefer it, as a matter of fact," Jan offered.

"Jan, honestly! What a worrier you are. Anybody would think you're my real mother, not my step, although I don't know of too many real mothers who cluck and hover like you do," she added with a grin.

"Okay, so I cluck and hover. Sue me," Jan muttered, crossing her arms over her chest.

"If you say another word about something's being wrong, I'll scream bloody murder. Nothing's wrong, believe me, aside from the usual things that always are, and you know all about those."

"You didn't go to see Brad?" Jan asked.

"No. Do you think I should have?"

Jan shrugged. "I don't know. It might not be a bad idea. Why don't you call him?"

"Jan . . ."

"All right, all right. I'll mind my own business," Jan said and, giving her a perfunctory kiss on the nose, slipped out the door. Kim fixed herself some soup and a grilled cheese sandwich, then went upstairs to her room. She sat down at her desk, took out a piece of stationery, and wrote on the top, *"Dear Mom."*

Okay, now what? *"Dear Mom, I never know what to say to you? I feel like we're strangers? I wish we could be close, but I'm afraid it's too late? Dear Mom, I'll never forgive you for leaving me when you did, for only thinking about yourself, and your own needs, when you should have thought about me, and mine, as well? Dear Mom, if only you could be like my stepmother, I could love you a lot?"*

A tear fell on the paper. She brushed it away and wrote, *"I was so happy when I* read your letter saying you were thinking of coming out here for opening night. . . ."

A good start. Next?

"But, unfortunately (or fortunately, depending on how you look at it), I'm not going to be in the play. Sanders has decided to give the part to someone else. Oh, by the way, he's the coach for the drama club, and we used to be friends. I'm not sure if we are anymore. All of which brings me to a question. Could you come, anyway? Because, if you could, I was thinking it would be great for us to spend a few days together, just the two of us. If you could fit it in, so could I. I'm going to have some time available starting pretty soon, and I can't think of anything I'd rather do with it than spend it with you.

Twenty·five

"You'll be relieved to know that you check out completely normal," Dr. Freed said, smiling across the desk at her. Kim let out her breath in a rush. She was relieved, only she couldn't help wondering. If there was nothing physically wrong with her, why did she keep getting headaches and walk around feeling so crummy all the time?

"If there's nothing wrong with her, what's causing these headaches?" her father asked, putting her thoughts into words.

"Whatever it is, it's not physiological as far as I can tell," Dr. Freed replied. It was the wrong thing to say to her father.

"You can't find anything on any of those tests you did. So, rather than admit you don't know, you'll resort to the convenient catchall and tell us Kim has psychological problems?" he declared.

Kim thought Dr. Freed would have a fit,

but she just smiled blithely at him and said with equanimity, "Don't put words into my mouth, Sam."

"So, there's nothing wrong with me then?" Kim put in.

The doctor shook her head. "Nothing that showed up on any of those tests or during the examination I gave you. In my opinion you're overtired, under a lot of tension and stress. You're going to have to do something about that, Kim."

"What do you suggest, Doc?" Kim asked.

"Cut down on some of those things you're doing, find some time to relax and enjoy yourself. Get out and have some fun!"

"Fun? That's what you're prescribing, Doc? *Fun?*" Kim laughed.

"Want me to write it out for you on an RX form so you can take it to the drugstore to be filled?"

"No, I think I'll remember it. It just so happens I have a best friend whose religion is fun. The thing is, it's been so long since I've had any, I'm not sure I remember *how*."

"Oh, you'll pick it up in no time," Dr. Freed assured her.

"Well, anyway, I'm relieved to hear I'm not suffering from some rare disease or something."

"Only now you're going to have to do something to alleviate the situation, and that's not going to be easy," Dr. Freed said, verbalizing her thoughts. Kim nodded. It was a little overwhelming to realize that, after sixteen years of being one type of person, she was going to have to transform herself into a whole other type.

"Well, I'm glad *that's* over!" she said to Jan and her father when they were driving home. "Now all I have to do is find out how to have fun. Fun, whatever *that* is! Wish you *could* pick it up at the drugstore. That'd make it easier. Jodi will be beside herself with joy to learn that her diagnosis of my problem and the doctor's coincide. She keeps telling me I ought to go out and have fun."

"Why don't the three of us take a little vacation after school is over in June?" her father said, pulling up at a traffic light.

"I don't have any vacation time coming, Sam," Jan said.

"And I can't go on a vacation. I'll just be starting work," Kim added.

Her father glanced at her in the rearview mirror. "That again?"

"Yes, that again, Daddy. I *do* want to work this summer. Even if something happens, and that job doesn't come through at Jan's office, I want to work!"

"You heard what Dr. Freed said. Fun, not work. I wish you'd forget all this nonsense about working, baby."

"And *I* wish you'd let her decide for herself whether she wants to spend the summer working or having fun!" Jan smiled when she said it, but you could tell she was dead serious. He looked nonplussed, but he didn't say a word. Jan gave his arm a pat. "Sam, she's not your little girl anymore. Time to let go."

"That's just it. I can't," he said mournfully. "She's all I have, my only daughter. I've been dreading this moment for years. Do you know that?"

"Daddy, daughters grow up, but they stay daughters," Kim said. "You put a lot of time and effort into me, into bringing me up, and you did a terrific job, and now you ought to have enough faith in me, and the job you did, to trust me to take it from here. I can do it, Daddy, if only you'll let me."

A big red truck pulled up alongside, and a cute guy in a baseball cap winked and smiled at her. She smiled back. "All right, I get the message," her father sighed, shaking his head. "Look at that. Never thought I'd see the day. My little girl flirting with truck drivers."

"Could I borrow the car?" Kim asked Jan when they got home.

"Going somewhere?" Jan said gleefully, handing her the keys.

"I was thinking of paying a certain person a visit."

"Does she mean Brad?" her father asked Jan.

"I don't know. Ask her," Jan replied.

"I would, only I'm afraid, now that she's all grown up, a grownup woman, independent, on her own, she'll tell me to mind my own business."

"Oh, Daddy! You're really milking it," Kim laughed.

"Don't be impatient with me, baby. People don't change overnight. I've been Daddy for such a long time, it's going to take me a while to get used to not being him anymore," he said sadly.

She smiled at him. "That's just it. You'll always be Daddy. To *me*, anyway. Growing up doesn't mean changing into somebody else. I want to be independent and on my own, but I don't want to be fatherless. There *is* a difference, you know."

"Very reassuring!" he called after her as she headed out the door to the car. "My daughter, the star, just turned into a grown woman in front of my eyes," she heard him say to Jan.

"What are your feelings on the subject of adoption, Sam?" she heard Jan reply.

Twenty-six

Kim pulled up in front of the big white house on the hill, the house that had the most spectacular view in the valley (that was, on days when the smog didn't obscure it completely). It was an old house and had originally been lived in by a famous silent-movie mogul. Now it was lived in by a future superstar.

She knocked on the front door. No one came to answer it. It wasn't surprising. Music blared from the house — not one record, but three, each one turned up full-volume. She tried the doorknob. The door opened, and she walked in. Brad's family was fearless. They never bothered to lock their doors.

The music was deafening. She could feel it reverberating inside her head. The Beatles, the Who, and Eric Clapton. Well, anyway, someone had great taste. A surfboard was propped up against the wall of the entryway.

She nearly walked right into a ten-speed bicycle. Eustace bounded at her out of nowhere, leaped up, put his paws on her shoulders, and started licking her face.

"Take me to your leader!" she told him. Tail wagging furiously, he led her into the living room. Lying on his back on the floor with his feet propped up on the piano bench, playing his twelve-string guitar and singing softly to himself, Bradley E. Berson was listening to the Beatles' "Abbey Road" album.

"I was in the neighborhood. Thought I'd drop in," she informed him. Not an original opening line, but it was all she could come up with on the spur of the moment. He scrambled to his feet and stood there looking at her. "Aren't you going to say hi . . . or something?" she added.

He picked up an album off the floor and held it out to her. "It's yours. Mine's got half the cover missing. Remember? Eustace ate it for dinner that time?"

She took the album from him. "Eustace always *did* have unusual eating habits," she said for lack of something better and tried a smile. His face didn't change expression. *Okay, next?* she thought, the smile slipping. Upstairs somewhere somebody yelled, "Who's got my synthesizer?" It sounded like Brad's brother Brett, but it could have been one of his other brothers — he had four. How about just playing it straight? It would save time, and maybe it would work better. She thought of what Jan had said about letting her feelings out and saying what she felt, and she murmured, "I wasn't really in the neighborhood. I came on purpose, because I wanted to apologize for yesterday. I had no idea the game was so important to you, or I never would have suggested skipping it and just going to the dance."

"It's okay. Forget it. Uh, listen, I've got to go somewhere. . . ." he mumbled, looking around the room at everything but her.

"No, it's *not* okay. Really, it isn't. Something occurred to me yesterday after we had that fight. I've really been pretty selfish, but I never realized it till now. I've been so involved in thinking about myself, and my own problems, I never thought about you and how you felt. You're always so good to me, always letting me have my way, doing whatever I want to do. I guess I got kind of spoiled, know what I mean? I took it for granted that game didn't really mean all that much to you, and . . ." she trailed off.

"And it doesn't," he said.

"It doesn't?"

"No. I hate basketball. You know that."

"Well then, why . . .?"

"Look, it was just one more thing to add to the list. One more time you canceled out on me. You keep saying it's because you have to study, and you have so much work to do, but, hey, I'm not *that* out of it. After a while I start getting the message, know what I mean? You know what hurts the most?

Knowing you lied to me. We never lied to one another, Kim. If you want to break it off, the least you could do is level. Come right out and say it. Don't make up excuses for not being with me. You owe me that much."

For a moment she just stood there staring at him, at a loss to know what he meant. Eustace sidled up to her and rubbed against her leg, tail wagging, gazing up at her, his eyes filled with adoration. How could Brad think that? It didn't seem possible. She had always thought they had such a completely open and honest relationship. Yet he had misconstrued everything completely, and she hadn't even been aware that he had. Jodi said he wasn't as confident as he acted. Maybe she was right. Maybe, just maybe, he was human and had weaknesses like everyone else. It was possible that, if she did, so might he. Had she expected too much of *him* too? Had she thought he was Mr. Perfect, and his one and only failing was always being late?

"I never lied to you," she said. "How could you think I would?"

"You're lying right now!" he shouted at her. "You tell me you're staying home to study for the SATs. Then you go to the beach with Jodi. You give me the same story the next day. You're studying, right? Then go out with your old man. Listen, I may not be in your league in the brains department, but I'm not an idiot. I know when I'm being conned. Knowing how your old man feels about me, that he's always after you to break up with me, naturally I have to come to the conclusion that he's gotten to you. He's got enough influence over you. I'm amazed he hasn't before *this*!"

"I don't believe you're saying these things," she said, choking on the words. "How could you think that? How *could* you? If you don't know by now how much I love you, you never will. And if you don't know I wouldn't lie, *especially* to you, you don't know me at all. My father influences me, sure, in a lot of ways, but never where you're concerned. I'm sorry that he doesn't approve, that he doesn't know you better, the way *I* know you, but however he feels about you, about *us*, doesn't influence me. I still feel the same. I guess, if you could think otherwise, we haven't got as good a relationship as I thought," she added, turning away. He came after her, put his hand on her arm to stop her from leaving. "Let me go!" she sobbed, trying to break free.

Kim, I'm sorry. I just wasn't seeing things clearly. My emotions got in the way. I know darn well none of that is true. I don't know why I said it. God, all I know is I love you, and I want us to be together!"

Eustace forced himself between them and looked up at her as if to say, "I love you, too!" She couldn't help laughing. "At least *he* understand me. What are you apologizing for? You have nothing to be sorry about. I'm the one who ought to be sorry," she said to Brad. "I got my priorities mixed up. I forgot the most important thing. *You!*"

"No, us!"

"I love you!" she exclaimed. She had never realized it before, but he was vulnerable, too.

The phone rang. Brad picked it up and said, "Brad Berson here. I can't come to the phone right now, but if you'll leave your name and message at the sound of the beep, I'll get back to you. *BEEP!*"

A girl's voice said, "This is Sherry, Bradley dear. Remember me — Stella? And I know you're there, so don't try to con me. The message was okay up to the beep. You're supposed to be here rehearsing *Streetcar*, remember? I know you have a propensity for being late, but this is ridiculous!"

Before Brad could reply, Kim took the phone out of his hand and said, "This is Kim Stanton speaking. Kimberly Stanton, otherwise known as Brad's girlfriend? Yeah, *that* Kimberly Stanton! So, listen, Sherry, or Stella, or whoever you are. I wouldn't hang around waiting if I were you. Brad's not going to be able to make it. He's a little tied up — like, say, for fifty or sixty years. That's kind of a looong time to wait, so take my advice and *don't!*"

"Fifty or sixty years?" Brad said, breaking up.

She put down the phone. "Yeah, give or take a year or two. I'm planning on this being a long-term relationship." She moved

170

into his arms, wound her arms around his neck, and before he could say another word, kissed him. It wasn't a platonic kiss.

"Kim?" he gasped, coming up for air. "Is that *you*?"

"Better believe it!" she laughed and kissed him again. "The one, the only, the inimitable Kim Stanton, original *ex*-overachiever of the year . . . lately known as Miss Perfect, may she rest in peace!"

WILDFIRE®

Move from one breathtaking romance to another with the #1 Teen Romance line in the country!

NEW WILDFIRES! $1.95 each

- ☐ MU32539-6 **BLIND DATE** Priscilla Maynard
- ☐ MU32541-8 **NO BOYS?** McClure Jones
- ☐ MU32538-8 **SPRING LOVE** Jennifer Sarasin
- ☐ MU31930-2 **THAT OTHER GIRL** Conrad Nowels

BEST-SELLING WILDFIRES! $1.95 each

- ☐ MU31981-7 **NANCY AND NICK** Caroline B. Cooney
- ☐ MU32313-X **SECOND BEST** Helen Cavanagh
- ☐ MU31849-7 **YOURS TRULY, LOVE, JANIE** Ann Reit
- ☐ MU31566-8 **DREAMS CAN COME TRUE** Jane Claypool Miner
- ☐ MU32369-5 **HOMECOMING QUEEN** Winifred Madison
- ☐ MU31261-8 **I'M CHRISTY** Maud Johnson
- ☐ MU30324-4 **I'VE GOT A CRUSH ON YOU** Carol Stanley
- ☐ MU32361-X **THE SEARCHING HEART** Barbara Steiner
- ☐ MU31710-5 **TOO YOUNG TO KNOW** Elisabeth Ogilvie
- ☐ MU32430-6 **WRITE EVERY DAY** Janet Quin-Harkin
- ☐ MU30956-0 **THE BEST OF FRIENDS** Jill Ross Klevin

Scholastic Inc.,
P.O. Box 7502, 2932 E. McCarty Street, Jefferson City, MO 65102
Please send me the books I have checked above. I am enclosing $_____
(please add $1.00 to cover shipping and handling). Send check or money order—
no cash or C.O.D.'s please.

Name _____

Address_____

City_____ State/Zip_____

Please allow four to six weeks for delivery. 9/83